THROUGH OTHER EYES

THROUGH OTHER EYES

ANIMAL STORIES BY WOMEN

EDITED BY
IRENE ZAHAVA

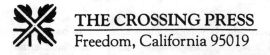

THE CROSSING PRESS
Freedom, California 95019

Grateful acknowledgement is made for permission to use the following previously published material:

"Am I Blue," by Alice Walker. From *Living By The Word*, by Alice Walker. Copyright © 1988 by Alice Walker. Reprinted by permission of Harcourt Brace Jovanovich.

"The Author of the Acacia Seeds and Other Extracts from the *Journal of the Association of Therolinguistics*," by Ursula K. Le Guin. Copyright © 1974 by Ursula K. Le Guin. Reprinted by permission of the author and the author's agent, Virginia Kidd.

"The Bear," excerpted from *Three Summers*, by Yvonne Pepin. Copyright © 1986 by Yvonne Pepin. Reprinted by permission of Shameless Hussy Press.

"The Donkey," excerpted from *Joanna and Ulysses, A Tale*, by May Sarton. Copyright © 1963 by May Sarton. Reprinted by permission of W.W. Norton & Company, Inc.

"He Was A Good Lion," excerpted from *West With The Night*, by Beryl Markham. Copyright © 1942, 1983 by Beryl Markham. Published by North Point Press and reprinted by permission.

"Homer-Snake," by Lou V. Crabtree. From *Sweet Hollow*, by Lou V. Crabtree. Copyright © 1984 by Lou V. Crabtree. Reprinted by permission of Louisiana State University Press.

"In Praise of Creeping Things," by Cathy Cockrell. From *A Simple Fact*, by Cathy Cockrell. Copyright © 1987 by Cathy Cockrell and reprinted by permission of the author.

"I've Finally Been Accepted By A Gorilla," excerpted from *Gorillas In The Mist*, by Dian Fossey. Copyright © 1983 by Dian Fossey. Reprinted by permission of Houghton Mifflin Company.

"The Muskrat," excerpted from *Pilgrim At Tinker Creek*, by Annie Dillard. Copyright © 1974 by Annie Dillard. Reprinted by permission of Harper & Row, Publishers, Inc.

"An Old Woman and Her Cat," by Doris Lessing. From *Stories*, by Doris Lessing. Copyright © 1972 by Doris Lessing. Reprinted by permission of Alfred A. Knopf, Inc.

"One Whale, Singing," by Keri Hulme. From *The Windeater/Te Kaihau*, by Keri Hulme. Copyright © 1986 by Keri Hulme. Reprinted by permission of George Braziller, Inc.

"Telepathic Rein," by Lou Robinson. Copyright © 1988 by Lou Robinson. Reprinted by permission of *The Quarterly*, #7 (story appeared as "Under the Apron that Held the Oracular Snake").

"Who Has Lived from A Child with Chickens," by Janet Kauffman. From *Places In The World A Woman Could Walk*, by Janet Kauffman. Copyright © 1981, 1983 by Janet Kauffman. Reprinted by permission of Alfred A. Knopf, Inc.

Cover art, "Allies," by Susan Seddon Boulet
Cover design by Duke Houston
Book design and production by Martha Waters
  text in Kennerly Oldstyle 11/12.5, titles in Garamond Antiqua

Printed in the U.S.A.

Library of Congress
Library of Congress Cataloging-in-Publication Data

Through other eyes : animal stories by women / edited by Irene Zahava
    p.   cm.
  ISBN 0-89594-315-8 :   ISBN 0-89594-314-X (pbk.) :
  1. Animals--Literary collections.   2. American prose literature-
  -Women authors.   3. English prose literature--Women authors.
  I. Zahava, Irene.
  PS648.A5T4 1988
  823'.008'036--dc19   88-23780
                                                            CIP

for Marty

Contents

Preface

I was not raised among animals. As a city-bred child I had the occasional pet goldfish or turtle, my family went on outings to The Bronx Zoo, but there was never any real connection between myself and an animal. In the past few years this has begun to change. I flatter myself that I share a unique bond with my calico cat and that ours is a mutually satisfying relationship. But is it?

Two years ago, when I read Alice Walker's essay "Am I Blue?" I was forced to challenge many assumptions I had held about animals. Walker describes the eloquently communicated messages she came to recognize in the eyes of a large white horse named Blue. After reading her words I felt compelled to push deeper toward an understanding of the ways in which the fate of humans and of animals is inextricably intertwined.

I turned to a number of women writers, looking for some of the ways other women have opened themselves to receive messages, and to learn lessons, from animals. The result of that search is this anthology: a collection of stories in which the integrity, dignity and individuality of animals is celebrated.

Through these stories I've begun to understand the patience and subtlety that is required of those who wish to observe animals without putting them under observation; and I've become more aware of the hard work ahead for all of us if we are to see a time when true communication, interaction and sharing takes place between ourselves and the animal world.

Irene Zahava
June, 1988

Am I Blue?

*"Aint these tears in these eyes tellin' you?"**

ALICE WALKER

*F*or about three years my companion and I rented a small house
in the country that stood on the edge of a large meadow that appeared to run from the end of our deck straight into the mountains. The mountains, however, were quite far away, and between us and them there was, in fact, a town. It was one of the
many pleasant aspects of the house that you never really were
aware of this.

It was a house of many windows, low, wide, nearly floor to
ceiling in the living room, which faced the meadow, and it was
from one of these that I first saw our closest neighbor, a large
white horse, cropping grass, flipping its mane, and ambling
about—not over the entire meadow, which stretched well out of
sight of the house, but over the five or so fenced-in acres that

---

were next to the twenty-odd that we had rented. I soon learned that the horse, whose name was Blue, belonged to a man who lived in another town, but was boarded by our neighbors next door. Occasionally, one of the children, usually a stocky teen-ager, but sometimes a much younger girl or boy, could be seen riding Blue. They would appear in the meadow, climb up on his back, ride furiously for ten or fifteen minutes, then get off, slap Blue on the flanks, and not be seen again for a month or more.

There were many apple trees in our yard, and one by the fence that Blue could almost reach. We were soon in the habit of feeding him apples, which he relished, especially because by the middle of summer the meadow grasses—so green and succulent since January—had dried out from lack of rain, and Blue stumbled about munching the dried stalks half-heartedly. Sometimes he would stand very still just by the apple tree, and when one of us came out he would whinny, snort loudly, or stamp the ground. This meant, of course: I want an apple.

It was quite wonderful to pick a few apples, or collect those that had fallen to the ground overnight, and patiently hold them, one by one, up to his large, toothy mouth. I remained as thrilled as a child by his flexible dark lips, huge, cubelike teeth that crunched the apples, core and all, with such finality, and his high, broad-breasted *enormity;* beside which, I felt small indeed. When I was a child, I used to ride horses, and was especially friendly with one named Nan until the day I was riding and my brother deliberately spooked her and I was thrown, head first, against the trunk of a tree. When I came to, I was in bed and my mother was bending worriedly over me; we silently agreed that perhaps horseback riding was not the safest sport for me. Since then I have walked, and prefer walking to horseback riding—but I had forgotten the depth of feeling one could see in horses' eyes.

I was therefore unprepared for the expression in Blue's. Blue was lonely. Blue was horribly lonely and bored. I was not shocked that this should be the case; five acres to tramp by yourself, endlessly, even in the most beautiful of meadows—and his was—cannot provide many interesting events, and once rainy season turned to dry that was about it. No, I was shocked that I had forgotten that human animals and nonhuman animals can communicate quite well; if we are brought up around animals as children we take this for granted. By the time we are adults we no longer remember. However, the animals have not changed. They are in fact *completed* creations (at least they seem to be, so much more than we) who are not likely *to* change; it is their nature to express themselves. What else are they going to express? And they do. And, generally speaking, they are ignored.

After giving Blue the apples, I would wander back to the house, aware that he was observing me. Were more apples not forthcoming then? Was that to be his sole entertainment for the day? My partner's small son had decided he wanted to learn how to piece a quilt; we worked in silence on our respective squares as I thought . . .

Well, about slavery: about white children, who were raised by black people, who knew their first all-accepting love from black women, and then, when they were twelve or so, were told they must "forget" the deep levels of communication between themselves and "mammy" that they knew. Later they would be able to relate quite calmly, "My old mammy was sold to another good family." "My old mammy was _____ _____." Fill in the blank. Many more years later a white woman would say: "I can't understand these Negroes, these blacks. What do they want? They're so different from us."

And about the Indians, considered to be "like animals" by the "settlers" (a very benign euphemism for what they actually were), who did not understand their description as a compliment.

And about the thousands of American men who marry Japanese, Korean, Filipina, and other non-English-speaking women and of how happy they report they are, "*blissfully,*" until their brides learn to speak English, at which point the marriages tend to fall apart. What then did the men see, when they looked into the eyes of the women they married, before they could speak English? Apparently only their own reflections.

I thought of society's impatience with the young. "Why are

they playing the music so loud?" Perhaps the children have listened to much of the music of oppressed people their parents
danced to before they were born, with its passionate but soft
cries for acceptance and love, and they have wondered why their
parents failed to hear.

I do not know how long Blue had inhabited his five beautiful,
boring acres before we moved into our house; a year after we had
arrived—and had also traveled to other valleys, other cities,
other worlds—he was still there.

But then, in our second year at the house, something happened in Blue's life. One morning, looking out the window at the
fog that lay like a ribbon over the meadow, I saw another horse, a
brown one, at the other end of Blue's field. Blue appeared to be
afraid of it, and for several days made no attempt to go near. We
went away for a week. When we returned, Blue had decided to
make friends and the two horses ambled or galloped along together, and Blue did not come nearly as often to the fence underneath
the apple tree.

When he did, bringing his new friend with him, there was a
different look in his eyes. A look of independence, of self-
possession, of inalienable *horse*ness. His friend eventually became
pregnant. For months and months there was, it seemed to me, a
mutual feeling between me and the horses of justice, of peace. I
fed apples to them both. The look in Blue's eyes was one of
unabashed "this is *it*ness."

It did not, however, last forever. One day, after a visit to the
city, I went out to give Blue some apples. He stood waiting, or so
I thought, though not beneath the tree. When I shook the tree
and jumped back from the shower of apples, he made no move. I
carried some over to him. He managed to half-crunch one. The
rest he let fall to the ground. I dreaded looking into his
eyes—because I had of course noticed that Brown, his partner,
had gone—but I did look. If I had been born into slavery, and my
partner had been sold or killed, my eyes would have looked like
that. The children next door explained that Blue's partner had
been "put with him" (the same expression that old people used, I

had noticed, when speaking of an ancestor during slavery who had been impregnated by her owner) so that they could mate and she conceive. Since that was accomplished, she had been taken back by her owner, who lived somewhere else.

Will she be back? I asked.

They didn't know.

Blue was like a crazed person. Blue *was,* to me, a crazed person. He galloped furiously, as if he were being ridden, around and around his five beautiful acres. He whinnied until he couldn't. He tore at the ground with his hooves. He butted himself against his single shade tree. He looked always and always toward the road down which his partner had gone. And then, occasionally, when he came up for apples, or I took apples to him, he looked at me. It was a look so piercing, so full of grief, a look so *human,* I almost laughed (I felt too sad to cry) to think there are people who do not know that animals suffer. People like me who have forgotten, and daily forget, all that animals try to tell us. "Everything you do to us will happen to you; we are your teachers, as you are ours. We are one lesson" is essentially it, I think. There are those who never once have even considered animals' rights: those who have been taught that animals actually want to be used and abused by us, as small children "love" to be frightened, or women "love" to be mutilated and raped. . . . They are the great-grandchildren of those who honestly thought, because someone taught them this: "Women can't think," and "niggers can't faint." But most disturbing of all, in Blue's large brown eyes was a new look, more painful than the look of despair: the look of disgust with human beings, with life; the look of hatred. And it was odd what the look of hatred did. It gave him, for the first time, the look of a beast. And what that meant was that he had put up a barrier within to protect himself from further violence; all the apples in the world wouldn't change that fact.

And so Blue remained, a beautiful part of our landscape, very peaceful to look at from the window, white against the grass. Once a friend came to visit and said, looking out on the soothing view: "And it *would* have to be a *white* horse; the very image of freedom." And I thought, yes, the animals are forced to become for us merely "images" of what they once so beautifully expressed. And we are used to drinking milk from containers showing "contented" cows, whose real lives we want to hear nothing about, eating eggs and drumsticks from "happy" hens, and munching hamburgers advertised by bulls of integrity who seem to command their fate.

As we talked of freedom and justice one day for all, we sat down to steaks. I am eating misery, I thought, as I took the first bite. And spit it out.

He Was A Good Lion

BERYL MARKHAM

When I was a child, I spent all my days with the Nandi Murani, hunting barefooted, in the Rongai Valley, or in the cedar forests of the Mau Escarpment.

At first I was not permitted to carry a spear, but the Murani depended on nothing else.

You cannot hunt an animal with such a weapon unless you know the way of his life. You must know the things he loves, the things he fears, the paths he will follow. You must be sure of the quality of his speed and the measure of his courage. He will know as much about you, and at times make better use of it.

But my Murani friends were patient with me.

"Amin yut!" one would say, "what but a dik-dik will run like that? Your eyes are filled with clouds today, Lakweit!"

That day my eyes were filled with clouds, but they were young enough eyes and they soon cleared. There were other days and other dik-dik. There were so many things.

There were dik-dik and leopard, kongoni and warthog, buffalo, lion, and the "hare that jumps." There were many thousands
of the hare that jumps.

And there were wildebeest and antelope. There was the
snake that crawls and the snake that climbs. There were birds,
and young men like whips of leather, like rainshafts in the sun,
like spears before a singiri.

"Amin yut!" the young men would say, "that is no buffalo
spoor, Lakweit. Here! Bend down and look. Bend down and look
at this mark. See how this leaf is crushed. Feel the wetness of this
dung. Bend down and look so that you may learn!"

And so, in time, I learned. But some things I learned alone.

There was a place called Elkington's Farm by Kabete Station.
It was near Nairobi on the edge of the Kikuyu Reserve, and my
father and I used to ride there from town on horses or in a buggy,
and along the way my father would tell me things about Africa.

Sometimes he would tell me stories about the tribal
wars—wars between the Masai and the Kikuyu (which the
Masai always won), or between the Masai and the Nandi (which
neither of them ever won), and about their great leaders and their
wild way of life which, to me, seemed much greater fun than our
own. He would tell me of Lenana, the brilliant Masai ol-oiboni,
who prophesied the coming of the White Man, and of Lenana's
tricks and stratagems and victories, and about how his people
were unconquerable and unconquered—until, in retaliation
against the refusal of the Masai warriors to join the King's
African Rifles, the British marched upon the Native villages;
how, inadvertently, a Masai woman was killed, and how two
Hindu shopkeepers were murdered in reprisal by the Murani.
And thus, why it was that the thin, red line of Empire had grown
slightly redder.

He would tell me old legends sometimes about Mount
Kenya, or about the Menegai Crater, called the Mountain of
God, or about Kilimanjaro. He would tell me these things and I

would ride alongside and ask endless questions, or we would sit together in the jolting buggy and just think about what he had said.

One day, when we were riding to Elkington's, my father spoke about lions.

"Lions are more intelligent than some men," he said, "and more courageous than most. A lion will fight for what he has and for what he needs; he is contemptuous of cowards and wary of his equals. But he is not afraid. You can always trust a lion to be exactly what he is — and never anything else."

"Except," he added, looking more paternally concerned than usual, "that damned lion of Elkington's!"

The Elkington lion was famous within a radius of twelve miles in all directions from the farm, because, if you happened to be anywhere inside that circle, you could hear him roar when he was hungry, when he was sad, or when he just felt like roaring. If, in the night, you lay sleepless on your bed and listened to an intermittent sound that began like the bellow of a banshee trapped in the bowels of Kilimanjaro and ended like the sound of that same banshee suddenly at large and arrived at the foot of your bed, you knew (because you had been told) that this was the song of Paddy.

Two or three of the settlers in East Africa at that time had caught lion cubs and raised them in cages. But Paddy, the Elkington lion, had never seen a cage.

He had grown to full size, tawny, black-maned and muscular, without a worry or a care. He lived on fresh meat, not of his own killing. He spent his waking hours (which coincided with everybody else's sleeping hours) wandering through Elkington's fields and pastures like an affable, if apostrophic, emperor, a-stroll in the gardens of his court.

He thrived in solitude. He had no mate, but pretended indifference and walked alone, not toying too much with imaginings of the unattainable. There were no physical barriers to his freedom, but the lions of the plains do not accept into their respected fraternity an individual bearing in his coat the smell of men. So

Paddy ate, slept, and roared, and perhaps he sometimes dreamed, but he never left Elkington's. He was a tame lion, Paddy was. He was deaf to the call of the wild.

"I'm always careful of that lion," I told my father, "but he's really harmless. I have seen Mrs. Elkington stroke him."

"Which proves nothing," said my father. "A domesticated lion is only an unnatural lion—and whatever is unnatural is untrustworthy."

Whenever my father made an observation as deeply philosophical as that one, and as inclusive, I knew there was nothing more to be said.

I nudged my horse and we broke into a canter covering the remaining distance to Elkington's.

It wasn't a big farm as farms went in Africa before the First World War, but it had a very nice house with a large veranda on which my father, Jim Elkington, Mrs. Elkington, and one or two other settlers sat and talked with what to my mind was always unreasonable solemnity.

There were drinks, but beyond that there was a tea-table lavishly spread, as only the English can spread them. I have sometimes thought since of the Elkingtons' tea-table—round, capacious, and white, standing with sturdy legs against the green vines of the garden, a thousand miles of Africa receding from its edge.

It was a mark of sanity, I suppose, less than of luxury. It was evidence of the double debt England still owes to ancient China for her two gifts that made expansion possible—tea and gunpowder.

But cakes and muffins were no fit bribery for me. I had pleasures of my own then, or constant expectations. I made what niggardly salutations I could bring forth from a disinterested memory and left the house at a gait rather faster than a trot.

As I scampered past the square hay shed a hundred yards or so behind the Elkington house, I caught sight of Bishon Singh whom my father had sent ahead to tend our horses.

I think the Sikh must have been less than forty years old

then, but his face was never any indication of his age. On some days he looked thirty and on others he looked fifty, depending on the weather, the time of day, his mood, or the tilt of his turban. If he had ever disengaged his beard from his hair and shaved the one and clipped the other, he might have astonished us all by looking like one of Kipling's elephant boys, but he never did either, and so, to me at least, he remained a man of mystery, without age or youth, but burdened with experience, like the wandering Jew.

He raised his arm and greeted me in Swahili as I ran through the Elkington farmyard and out toward the open country.

Why I ran at all or with what purpose in mind is beyond my answering, but when I had no specific destination I always ran as fast as I could in the hope of finding one—and I always found it.

I was within twenty yards of the Elkington lion before I saw him. He lay sprawled in the morning sun, huge, black-maned, and gleaming with life. His tail moved slowly, stroking the rough grass like a knotted rope end. His body was sleek and easy, making a mould where he lay, a cool mould, that would be there when he had gone. He was not asleep; he was only idle. He was rusty-red, and soft, like a strokable cat.

I stopped and he lifted his head with magnificent ease and stared at me out of yellow eyes.

I stood there staring back, scuffling my bare toes in the dust, pursing my lips to make a noiseless whistle—a very small girl who knew about lions.

Paddy raised himself then, emitting a little sigh, and began to contemplate me with a kind of quiet premeditation, like that of a slow-witted man fondling an unaccustomed thought.

I cannot say that there was any menace in his eyes, because there wasn't, or that his "frightful jowls" were drooling, because they were handsome jowls and very tidy. He did sniff the air, though, with what impressed me as being close to audible satisfaction. And he did not lie down again.

I remembered the rules that one remembers. I did not run. I walked very slowly, and I began to sing a defiant song.

"Kali coma Simba sisi," I sang, "Asikari yoti ni udari!—Fierce like the lion are we, Askari all are brave!"

I went in a straight line past Paddy when I sang it, seeing his eyes shine in the thick grass, watching his tail beat time to the metre of my ditty.

"Twendi, twendi—ku pigana—piga aduoi—piga sana!—Let us go, let us go—to fight—beat down the enemy! Beat hard, beat hard!"

What lion would be unimpressed with the marching song of the King's African Rifles?

Singing it still, I took up my trot toward the rim of the low hill which might, if I were lucky, have Cape gooseberry bushes on its slopes.

The country was grey-green and dry, and the sun lay on it closely, making the ground hot under my bare feet. There was no sound and no wind.

Even Paddy made no sound, coming swiftly behind me.

What I remember most clearly of the moment that followed are three things—a scream that was barely a whisper, a blow that struck me to the ground, and, as I buried my face in my arms and felt paddy's teeth close on the flesh of my leg, a fantastically bobbing turban, that was Bishon Singh's turban, appear over the edge of the hill.

I remained conscious, but I closed my eyes and tried not to be. It was not so much the pain as it was the sound.

The sound of Paddy's roar in my ears will only be duplicated, I think, when the doors of hell slip their wobbly hinges, one day, and give voice and authenticity to the whole panorama of Dante's poetic nightmares. It was an immense roar that encompassed the world and dissolved me in it.

I shut my eyes very tight and lay still under the weight of Paddy's paws.

Bishon Singh said afterward that he did nothing. He said he had remained by the hay shed for a few minutes after I ran past him, and then, for no explainable reason, had begun to follow me. He admitted, though, that, a little while before, he had seen Paddy go in the direction I had taken.

The Sikh called for help, of course, when he saw the lion meant to attack, and a half-dozen of Elkington's syces had come running from the house. Along with them had come Jim Elkington with a rawhide whip.

Jim Elkington, even without a rawhide whip, was very impressive. He was one of those enormous men whose girths alone seem to preclude any possibility of normal movement, much less of speed. But Jim had speed—not to be loosely compared with lightning, but rather like the speed of something spherical and smooth and relatively irresistible, like the cannon balls of the Napoleonic Wars. Jim was, without question, a man of considerable courage, but in the case of my Rescue From the Lion, it was, I am told, his momentum rather than his bravery for which I must forever be grateful.

It happened like this as Bishon Singh told it;

"I am resting against the walls of the place where hay is kept and first the large lion and then you, Beru, pass me going toward the open field, and a thought comes to me that a lion and a young girl are strange company, so I follow. I follow to the place where the hill that goes up becomes the hill that goes down, and where it goes down deepest I see that you are running without much thought in your head and the lion is running behind you with many thoughts in his head, and I scream for everybody to come very fast.

"Everybody comes very fast, but the large lion is faster than anybody, and he jumps on your back and I see you scream but I hear no scream. I only hear the lion, and I begin to run with everybody, and this includes Bwana Elkington, who is saying a great many words I do not know and is carrying a long kiboko which he holds in his hand and is meant for beating the large lion.

"Bwana Elkington goes past me the way a man with lighter legs and fewer inches around his stomach might go past me, and he is waving the long kiboko so that it whistles over all of our heads like a very sharp wind, but when we get close to the lion it comes to my mind that that lion is not of the mood to accept a kiboko.

"He is standing with the front of himself on your back, Beru, and you are bleeding in three or five places, and he is roaring. I do not believe Bwana Elkington could have thought that that lion at that moment would consent to being beaten, because the lion was not looking the way he had ever looked before when it was necessary for him to be beaten. He was looking as if he did not wish to be disturbed by a kiboko, or the Bwana, or the syces, or Bishon Singh, and he was saying so in a very large voice.

"I believe that Bwana Elkington understood this voice when he was still more than several feet from the lion, and I believe the Bwana considered in his mind that it would be the best thing not to beat the lion just then, but the Bwana when he runs very fast is like the trunk of a great baobob tree rolling down a slope, and it seems that because of this it was not possible for him to explain the thought of his mind to the soles of his feet in a sufficient quickness of time to prevent him from rushing much closer to the lion than in his heart he wished to be.

"And it was this circumstance, as I am telling it," said Bishon Singh, "which in my considered opinion made it possible for you to be alive, Beru."

"Bwana Elkington rushed at the lion then, Bishon Singh?"

"The lion, as of the contrary, rushed at Bwana Elkington," said Bishon Singh. "The lion deserted you for the Bwana, Beru. The lion was of the opinion that his master was not in any honest way deserving of a portion of what he, the lion, had accomplished in the matter of fresh meat through no effort by anybody except himself."

Bishon Singh offered this extremely reasonable interpretation with impressive gravity, as if he were expounding the Case For the Lion to a chosen jury of Paddy's peers.

"Fresh meat". . . I repeated dreamily, and crossed my fingers.

"So then what happened . . . ?"

The Sikh lifted his shoulders and let them drop again. "What could happen, Beru? The lion rushed for Bwana Elkington, who in his turn rushed from the lion, and in so rushing did not keep in his hand the long kiboko, but allowed it to fall upon the ground, and in accomplishing this the Bwana was free to ascend a very fortunate tree, which he did."

"And you picked me up, Bishon Singh?"

He made a little dip with his massive turban. "I was happy with the duty of carrying you back to this very bed, Beru, and of advising your father, who had gone to observe some of Bwana Elkington's horses, that you had been moderately eaten by the large lion. Your father returned very fast, and Bwana Elkington some time later returned very fast, but the large lion has not returned at all."

The large lion had not returned at all. That night he killed a horse, and the next night he killed a yearling bullock, and after that a cow fresh for milking.

In the end he was caught and finally caged, but brought to no rendezvous with the firing squad at sunrise. He remained for years in his cage, which, had he managed to live in freedom with his inhibitions, he might never have seen at all.

It seems characteristic of the mind of man that the repression of what is natural to humans must be abhorred, but that what is natural to an infinitely more natural animal must be confined within the bounds of a reason peculiar only to men—more peculiar sometimes than seems reasonable at all.

Paddy lived, people stared at him and he stared back, and this went on until he was an old, old lion. Jim Elkington died, and Mrs. Elkington, who really loved Paddy, was forced, because of circumstances beyond her control or Paddy's, to have him shot by Boy Long, the manager of Lord Delamere's estates.

This choice of executioners was, in itself, a tribute to Paddy, for no one loved animals more or understood them better, or could shoot more cleanly than Boy Long.

But the result was the same to Paddy. He had lived and died in ways not of his choosing. He was a good lion. He had done what he could about being a tame lion. Who thinks it just to be judged by a single error?

I still have the scars of his teeth and claws, but they are very

small now and almost forgotten, and I cannot begrudge him his
moment.

Henderson

MEREDITH ROSE

*H*enderson is stuck. She is out there, I know where she is, but I can't help her. I didn't name her or number her, but it goes like this—Henderson, number nine hundred ninety-nine, and what in the world I would give just to set her free. I don't mean unlatch the gate after all the cows have been milked for the third and last time that day and it's already twelve-thirty at night. Nor do I want to free her from the milking parlor—no need for her to stand on the platform with five others of her kind, have her teats pulled and the machine slipped on and stay on until another machine says she's finished. Henderson's problem goes far deeper than the chance to run free in the winter wheat until we can round her up.

Henderson wants only what is right for her and that's why she acts the way she does. Three times a day she kicks the hell out of somebody's hands as they try to do their job and she protests having to do hers. It is a battle all of us have lost. Even if she lived in India her life would be no more pleasant. She could roam the streets, have a vague feeling of freedom with a little respect thrown in, but it wouldn't be the best answer.

All of us must do our job—that is known as the "work ethic." We must do our duty and if we do do it, then we are good. The same holds true for the cows. If they don't let loose their milk then they're fired. It's a serious charge. The meat wagon doesn't know the difference between Henderson or Polly or Saralynn, like we do. When the time comes, the truck rolls up to the weigh scale and it's all over.

The cows know this.

Henderson is a Holstein. All white except for a round black patch on her left side where her number is emblazoned, and she is small. A mere half ton in a world where fifteen hundred pounds is average. Her size makes her easy to pick on. Everyone loves to harass Henderson, though there were those of us, before her problem was fully understood, who treated her civilly, gently and with caution. For awhile she was only a number, 999, and that's what we called her. It added to her unsociable demeanor. Whenever she misbehaved we could spit out an oath and attach 999 to the end of it and feel better.

She remained a number until a few days after her first calf was born. That was when we brought her up to the milking parlor for her initiation into the world of dairy farming. As a brand new milking cow she had every right to kick. There was that first milking when she waited until almost all the other cows in her group had been milked. There were only six left, including her, and she waddled in at the end of the line, her afterbirth trailing behind her like a bride's wedding train. It took two kickguards and someone holding her tail before the machine could be put in place. After that, every time she walked inside the milking parlor she had a piece of fear in her eyes, a wild look that was so different from any of the other cows it made me wonder what demons she lived with; wild and jittery and it showed in the way she carried her head and moved her feet and scurried out of the milking parlor as soon as we opened the gate. Just a friendly pat on the rump sent her flying.

Some cows forced their personalities on us. Rick and Polly and Benga all made an effort to be recognized for various rea- sons — so slow, so friendly, so stubborn. Number 999 was so ner- vous. She was so nervous that when she kicked she got both back legs up at once, just a few inches, but enough to make her look like she was tap dancing if I was in a good mood during that milk- ing. Any cow like that deserved to be known so I looked up her number in the files and found out her name was Henderson.

I tried to be nice to her and get to know her better. Some days after work I went over to her shed to be with her, maybe say a few words, maybe not, but I never tried to get too close, though she did sniff me once. When I walked past her shed in a hurry I didn't notice anything, but those evenings when I stopped to visit I could tell something was wrong. Henderson seemed awkward. It wasn't how she looked, but how she acted that made her seem different. She never tussled over food or water like the other cows. She always sat in the corner away from the action and her jumps were so half-hearted.

Every few weeks the cows went into heat according to their cycle. Some of them mooed in the direction of heaven while others pranced about and ran back and forth in their sheds. Most of them liked to jump on each other. The first time I saw all of this activity I was embarrassed. Grown cows licking on each other and jumping on the back of one or the head of another. It was too much like real life to be ignored. Then I grasped the business end of it all. Everyone and every cow in the dairy was there to produce milk. The way we got the most milk was to make a cow pregnant and wait for her to bear a calf, and then col- lect all her milk three times a day until her level dropped off and she got pregnant again. This irreverent spying on the sex life of a cow was purely for economic reasons. I stood outside the gate with clipboard in hand jotting down who did what to whom and when. They were a brazen lot and didn't care who was watching. Henderson, like the other cows, got aroused every twenty-one days or so, but her heat was a quiet one without any fanfare.

And whenever she got enough gusto to jump she was usually off center. She'd try to jump on a cow's side or else she'd aim for the back and miss and end up looking the fool.

Even with all her anxiety she was a powerful animal who produced strange reactions in us. The kickguard milkers placed the metal bar on her as soon as she walked into the milking parlor. The petters stroked her udder and tried to calm her down. I was the type of milker who turned my head and closed my eyes and said, "Nice cow, nice cow," as she tried to walk on my hands.

My hands were nothing compared to her hooves. If I had finally attached the machine to all four teats, and she kicked it off and stood on one of the vacuum hoses, there was no amount of pushing or pulling or hitting that could get her to move her foot. We learned her ticklish spots though. There was a space between the cleft in her hoof that I could rub and when I did that she moved her foot in reflex. My hand was like an ornery gnat that buzzed around her hooves. She could swat at it with her tail or jab at it with her foot and when she connected, that old gnat went away for a few seconds. The kick happened suddenly. One moment I'd be whizzing down the line putting on machines and taking off machines—the next thing I knew my wrist and thumb had been smacked with a hammer.

What could make a cow so afraid I wondered. She had the perfect life—all the food she wanted to eat, all the water she wanted to drink, cool showers in the summer when it was so hot the flies didn't bother to buzz. She had companionship—at least fifty other cows in her group alone. Once a year she got her toe nails clipped and filed, and when her tail got all nasty and full of doo-doo we'd snip the ugly parts away. A doctor came to visit if anything was wrong with her. She had her own number, her own official history filed away in the computer. All of us knew who she was. We had a personal relationship with her, not like 1029 or 536—we didn't know who they were and we didn't care. But Henderson . . .

Some days, early in the morning, when the sun hadn't shown up yet, I'd bring in the first group. I clapped my hands and said the words that are supposed to stimulate a cow to stand up. They all made the effort, bones creaking, early morning farts and peeing and everything we might do when we first wake up except they weren't as discreet as you and me. I herded them toward the gate and out of the corner of my eye I saw Henderson, still on the ground, her back to me, trying to hide.

So, Henderson didn't like to be milked and I can't blame her. Three times, every day, she had to stop what she was doing and walk over to the milking parlor. She had to stand close together with a group of cows she didn't even like since they picked on her all the time. Then, when all the cows were packed in the corral we rang a bell that was designed to make them walk inside the milking parlor, six to the right side, six to the left. In the middle, between the two rows of cows, was the pit where the milkers worked. The floor was sunk a few feet so when the cows were all in place we were about eye level with their bellies. They faced the wall and had no idea what we were up to.

For all the unflattering qualities assigned to them, these animals were no fools. There were a few of them, like 1064 or 1083 who always made sure they were at the front of the line, but they refused to walk in all the way. The entrance on either side was wide enough for one whole cow to step inside. If 1064 felt like it, she simply stood at the front of the door and said to hell with it. We rang a bell that was hooked up to a long metal bar at the back of the corral. Whenever the bell sounded, the bar moved forward a bit and convinced the cows to move forward also. We rang the bell and told 1064 to get her butt inside and sometimes we pleaded and sometimes we were cruel. Never too cruel, just a twist of her tail or a squirt of water in her face was enough to motivate her, except for those days she kept her weight in one place and demonstrated how smart, or how stubborn, she could be. Finally, with the weight of forty-nine cows pushing and shoving behind her, 1064 took that one step up and walked to the end of her row with five other cows behind her all eager to get the whole thing over with.

About half way through the first group, Henderson showed

up in the middle of a row, sandwiched between two cows that had a good five hundred pounds on her. The radio blared, the vacuum pump and generator tried to drown out the radio, another milker and I tried to have a conversation above all that noise and if I wasn't paying attention my hand was on a Henderson teat and a hoof was on my hand. It didn't matter what radio station we listened to, or who was milking her—she kicked. And when she kicked there was nothing to do except glare at her ankles and wash the cow crap off my hand and rub my sore wrist.

Kicking was not her worst fault. About the time I realized what was truly wrong with her, a terrible thing happened. Her milk level dropped. She went from giving thirty liters a day to twenty-five and there was no reason. She wasn't pregnant or in heat or sick. Every month Boaz came to check the milk. He analyzed two hundred cows and Henderson's number sank to the bottom of his list. Only a few of us expressed any joy at the possible loss of Henderson. The rest of us encouraged her to do better and stop kicking. After the results of the milk check came in, the dairy manager tacked a list on the bulletin board with the numbers of the cows that were soon to be sold. Each month I scanned the list to see if 999 had been chosen. It didn't take long for her number to come up. I remember running out to her shed to tell her the bad news. She didn't have much time to shape up and become the cow she could be, the cow who gave lots of milk, bore beautiful calves, and didn't kick. On the day I told her what her current standing was and what options were available she didn't even care. She just poked at her food and in her typical Henderson fashion didn't bother to move when 437 peed on her accidentally.

She was hopeless and I was hopelessly attached to her, but that didn't matter either.

A couple of days later it was my turn to watch the cows to see who needed to be inseminated. I had the evening shift and I spent some extra time with Henderson's group. I studied her closely for any signs that might indicate why she was losing her milk. She had her ears back, but they weren't especially warm to the touch so she wasn't feverish. A few regulation flies rested in the corners of her eyes. That was it. All I saw was a perfectly normal cow, a tad on the small side. I walked to the gate and stared a good-bye in her direction. She stood some feet away looking at me with a blank expression. I turned to leave and saw something out of the corner of my eye. I looked again and saw a vision—I saw the real Henderson and I understood. I walked a few steps closer to get a better look and Henderson's problem became obvious. She wasn't a dairy cow—she was a physicist trapped in the body of a cow. She was a scientist and she was supposed to be wearing black horn rimmed glasses and a pocket calculator. She shouldn't have been standing there naked with nothing on but her hide. She needed a pair of polyester pants and a permanent press shirt with a plastic comb and two pens in the front left pocket. This was not an anthropomorphic fantasy—this was the truth.

The next day at work I told everyone. We walked out to look at Henderson and she had physicist written all over her. Everything became clear—all the kicking and trying to hide and her depressions. We understood and I wanted that to be some consolation to her. She didn't know we knew and even if she did there was nothing any of us could do. Renée Richards never had it as bad as Henderson did, standing there, ankle deep in cow shit, wanting only to study a table of logarithms and instead having to endure three milkings a day for the rest of her life.

Henderson's milk level continued to decrease. It was as if she was saying, If I can't be a physicist, then I just don't want to be. The meat wagon wasn't far off, but she didn't heed our warnings. Some of us talked to the manager and explained what Henderson's trouble was, in hopes of sparing her that tortuous walk onto the weigh scale and up the cement ramp that led to a waiting cattle truck. He told us that the best price wins, but none of us had the money to buy her.

The only thing Henderson had going for her at this point was luck. The next week a poor farmer came by. He wanted to buy a cow for his personal use, a cow that didn't give much milk, one he would milk by hand, not by machine. We had such an animal. The day he came to take her away we felt relief and sadness – we were sorry to see her go, but glad she wasn't heading to the butcher, and a couple of us were overjoyed that we wouldn't have to milk her anymore.

Henderson was a physicist, not a cow. It wasn't her fault she was born with the wrong genetic makeup. Now she had avoided death for awhile more. We thought this sale granted her a reprieve, though for all we knew her life was a living hell without the benefit of subatomic particles and the unity of oneness. But the decision had been made. This sale would be her best chance. So when the farmer had loaded her on his truck and asked if she kicked much, we all said, No, and waved good-bye.

Homer-Snake

LOU V. CRABTREE

Old Marth claimed all the blacksnakes as hers. She tongue-lashed the roving Murray boys, who went into people's barns and caught snakes and took them by their tails and cracked them like whips. This cracking broke the body of the snake and sometimes snapped off its head. It was terrible to see the Murray boys wring a snake around a few times, then give a jerk and off snap the head.

Old Marth lived in her cabin next to our cabin down in the hollow of the river hills. She pinned her gray hair with long wire hairpins. I watched her stick the wire hairpins into her hair with little flicks of the wrist. It hurt her head, I thought. Only when she was bothered did her hair escape the pins and fall in gray wisps about her face. Bud, my brother younger than I a few years, thought it his mission in life to trail me, to spy, and to report on me to Maw. Some things Bud would tell but not many. Only things on me. Bud said I told everything I knew. Maw said it, too. Because of this, Bud never let me trek over the hills with him.

He said, "She just can't keep from talking. She talks all along the trace. If you talk, you don't get to know anything."

Old Marth leaned down close to Bud. "Blacksnakes are best of friends. Come down to my house and I'll show you Homer-snake."

I had seen Homer-snake many times. Bud had, too. Homer had lived for years back of Old Marth's house in the corner of the outside rock chimney. A hole was visible, where for warmth Homer crawled in the winter.

I once asked Old Marth, "Did Homer-snake dig his hole by himself?"

Old Marth replied, "I expect it is a once frog hole."

What Old Marth told Bud next was not news to Bud or to me. We had both seen it a million times.

"Homer-snake likes milk to drink. I put out milk for him in his saucer every day. Best of all he likes cream, which I don't give him but ever once in a while. He might get too fat to go in his hole." Old Marth laughed, then fiercelike advanced close to Bud. "Don't you ever come to be tormenting blacksnakes. I'll be wastin' my breath if you come to be like them rovin' Murray boys. Come to my house soon and get better acquainted with my Homer-snake."

Old Marth wouldn't have liked what Bud was carrying around in his pocket. I asked him what the small white rocks were that looked like they were rolled in salt.

"Blacksnake eggs. I found them under a rock up the ridge."

Old Marth was always asking me to go home with her to spend the night. She never asked Bud. He tried to devil me behind Old Marth's back.

"How would you like to turn down your bed covers and there would be Old Homer all curled up warming your bed?"

Then I accused Bud of being jealous, and we got into one of our many spats until Maw moved in, saying, "Old Marth just don't like boys. She is suspecting on account of them Murray boys."

Bud never was known to give up. He used to slink around the house as I was leaving, and peep around the corner, and hiss, "Don't sit down on Homer-snake."

Behind Old Marth's house and up a little rocky path was her vegetable garden. To one side was her little barn where she kept her cow, some hens, and a red rooster. The rooster did not like Homer and gave him many a good flogging. He raked Homer with his spurs until Homer fled from the barn, leaving the rooster and hens alone.

Nevertheless, on the sly, Homer would steal into the barn where he unhinged his jaws and swallowed whole one of the hen's nice eggs. Then off he would sneak, toward the rocky path, where he knocked and banged himself against the rocks until the prongs on his ribs crushed the shell of the egg. Once I saw Homer with a huge knot along his body, and I rushed to Old Marth, alarmed.

Old Marth answered in a knowing way. "Most likely an egg. Could be a mouse or a baby rabbit. Homer-snake is having his dinner."

Once the Murray boys were out "rogueing"—knocking off apples and stealing eggs. Homer was in the warm hen's nest where the hen had just laid a nice egg. Homer liked the warmth and was nestling down and warming himself before swallowing the egg, which was sort of an ordeal for him. A rude hand, reaching into the nest, and pulling out Homer, let go quickly. Even the Murray boys didn't like surprises like Homer.

"Homer is my protection," cackled Old Marth as the Murray boys skirted her place, skulking about carrying an old sack they put their loot into. Old Marth guessed that the Murray boys were out to get Homer. Twice they were almost successful.

Homer loved to climb trees. There were young birds and other delights. He played hide and seek up in the sycamore tree down by the little springhouse. He climbed to the very tiptop and out of his snake eyes viewed the world. I liked to watch him hang like a string and swing in the sycamore tree.

On this particular day, Old Homer had left the sycamore and was up in the tree that had the squirrel's nest. It had once been a crow's nest, but the squirrels had taken over for the summer. In the winter they had a fine home in a hole just below the crow's nest.

Homer liked young squirrels almost as much as young rabbits. The Murray boys almost got Homer that time. They spotted him up in the tree that had the squirrel's nest. Climbing a tree was nothing to the Murray boys. They could climb to the top of any tree in the Hollow. Homer-snake was in a predicament. The leanest of the Murrays was coming right on up the tree with no problem. Homer couldn't see Old Marth anywhere. It would be too late in a minute. A rough hand would be reaching for him.

There were some small limbs, too small to hold the weight of a boy, and farther on, still smaller limbs that just possibly could hold up a snake. Out crawled Old Homer and with great care coiled himself round and round the smallest ones.

The Murray boy was plain mad. The limb would not hold up his weight. He ventured out as far as he could and leaned out and down and stretched his arm toward Homer.

"Shake him loose. Shake hard."

Round and round the tree looking up, calling louder and louder, went the rest of the boys until the red rooster brought together his pack of hens and they all set to cackling, which caused the hogs to trot around the pen, grunting. Just in time, out of the house, like a whirlwind, came Old Marth. The Murray boys knew to make themselves scarce and they hightailed it, except the one caught up in the tree who tried to skin down fast. Old Marth got hold of his hair and yanked him about, and when he left, he left a piece of his shirt with Old Marth.

Laughter floated backwards as the Murray boys hightailed it, putting distance between them and Old Marth's screeching.

"Rogues! Torments! Thieves!"

So Homer was saved this first time.

Another time, the Murray boys were watching Old Marth's house and knew she was away. They were walking around looking at the roots she had tied up to the rafters of her porch. They had been down to the hogpen and down to the springhouse and had drunk out of the gourd. They spied Homer, who was coming from the garden. He barely got halfway in his door when one of the Murrays got him by the tail, straining and tugging to pull him out. What they did not know was that no one, not anyone, can pull a snake out of his hole, once he gets part way in. The snake swells up and spreads his scales and each scale has a tiny muscle. The snake may be pulled into two parts, but he will never be moved. The Murray boys did not give up easy as they pulled and tugged.

"Pull harder. Yank him outa there."

Homer was about to come apart when he felt footsteps coming along on the ground. Old Marth, home early, came upon the scene and chased off the Murrays with a tongue-lashing they would remember. Homer-snake was saved the second time, but there was to be a third.

In the late summer, Homer got a new skin. He molted. He had a bad case of lassitude. Then his whole body was itching so he could not rest. His lips began to split and his eyes turned milky. He was milky-looking all over. He made trip after trip up into the garden, ate a big lunch of snails and bugs, and lazed back down over the rocky path.

One day there was his old skin beside the path in the rocks. Of course he knew all along what he was doing and just how to do it. He rubbed and rubbed himself against the rocks until his old skin loosened and he rolled it off wrong side out. Just like Bud shed his clothes.

Old Marth found the skin and tied it with several others to the rafters of her porch. When the wind rattled them, they scared me, but not Homer's old enemies, the Murrays.

Old Marth said to Bud after Homer shed his skin, "I will make you acquainted with the new Homer. Don't you like him? Ain't he handsome? Like a new gun barrel, he is."

With his new skin, Homer was so shiny and new, I think Bud almost liked him. Homer looked "spit shined," like Paw said about his shoes from his old army days.

Homer got along real well with the cow. She ignored him and never got ruffled if she came upon him suddenly. Homer only had to watch her feet. She did not care where she stepped. Four feet were a lot to watch and one day Homer got careless. One of the cow's feet came down hard on about three inches of Homer's tail. When Homer looked back, the end of his tail was broken off and sticking out of the mud in the cow's track. His beautiful tail. So for the rest of his life he went about trailing his blunted tail, and after a while he didn't seem to miss it.

Bud said, "I can always tell if it is Homer trailing through the sands and dust. Among the squiggles you can see where his old stepped-on tail went."

Down in the springhouse Old Homer guarded the milk crocks. He would curl around a crock like giving it a good hug-ging. Old Marth had to keep the lids weighted down with heavy rocks so Homer wouldn't knock the covers off and get in the milk.

Looking back, behind the springhouse, was a swath of daisies with bunches of red clover marked here and there, winding all the way to the top of the ridge. This swath was Homer-snake's special place. He liked to lie and rest and cool off among the daisies. He played all the way to the top of the ridge, got tired and slept, had lunch along the way, slithered down when he chose, spending the whole of a summer's day to arrive back home in the cool of the evening. The daisies gave Homer-snake a nice feeling.

The Murray boys were Homer's end. This was the third en-counter.

"All things have an end." Maw said later.

Maw sent me down to Old Marth's place to swap some quilt pieces. Going to her house was all right if I could locate Homer. Sitting on Homer or having him swing down from a rafter and touch me on the shoulder never got any less upsetting. But something bad was waiting for us all that day at Old Marth's place.

Homer was fat and lazy and full of cream.

"I'll put in a spoon of jelly for you, Homer." Old Marth put the jelly in Homer-snake's saucer and went on her way. She was going over the hill to visit and take a sample of the jelly.

Homer loved the jelly. Then I know he began feeling lonely. Loneliness led to carelessness. He failed to notice that everything was too quiet. The birds were quiet like the Murray boys were in the vicinity. The chickens were quiet like a hawk was circling. Homer decided to slip past the rooster and go into the barn to rest.

The Murray boys were out "funning" all day all over the hills. They were stirring up bees' nests beside the trace and getting people stung. They were running the cows so they wouldn't let their milk down. They were riding the steers and tormenting the bull.

They saw Old Marth going over the ridge and grinned at each other and jammed down their old hats over their ears and hitched up their britches. Preparing themselves. Preparing to steal eggs out of the hens' nests, they went into the barn. Bud saw it all and told Maw.

Maw said to me, "There is such a thing as keeping your mouth shut."

Bud was watching the Murray boys that day. He had trailed them and watched from the far edge of the woods on the top of the hill. Bud was always watching. I saw him in the plum grove. He was no partner in what happened.

The Murray boys went into the barn with their everlasting sack, stayed a few minutes, rushed out toward the hogpen, pitched the sack, and whatever was in it, over to the hogs. Then they laughed and shouted and hightailed it.

I saw it. Bud saw it. I ran to tell Maw.

"They threw the sack and Homer in it into the hogpen. The hogs will eat up Homer." I was running, screaming wild, and blubbering.

I was so excited with telling the tale that I had not had time to feel sorry for Homer. The hogpen was one place Homer never fooled around. Even Homer knew that hogs ate up blacksnakes.

Bud had come up. "How are you going to keep her from blab-bing?" Bud thought he was the world's best at keeping his mouth shut. He gloried in keeping secrets.

I wanted to talk about what I saw, and I wanted to bring it up ever afterwards and keep asking questions. There was so much to wonder about.

"She will tell her guts," Bud said.

"Let Homer bide," was what Maw said to me and meant it. I could tell for her mouth was a straight line across.

Old Marth came home, missed Homer, and looked every-where. Bud and I stood around and watched her. Her eyes were on the ground looking for some sign, trying to find a trail.

I mooned around and was about sick seeing Old Marth with her graying hair stringing and wisping about her face. Until one day, Old Marth said, "If Homer were alive, he would show up. I know when to give up hopes. I resign myself."

Determined not to let anything slip about Homer, for a while, it helped to clap both hands over my mouth when questions began popping in my head. I didn't want ever to be the first one to tell about Homer being eaten by the—I must not say it now.

Maw kept saying, "Let it bide a while."

Old Marth came back to our house to churn. Her hair like a cap was pinned up with long hairpins. Maw required neat hair around the butter, for a hair found in the butter made a bad tale up and down the Hollow.

I kept holding both hands over my mouth to keep from telling until one day Old Marth noticed and said, "You are acting funny." Turning to Maw, she said, "The child is sick. Goes around all the time about to vommick holding her hands over her mouth. Just might be she is wormy and needs a dose."

I wasn't sick. Maw knew it. Bud knew it.

Days went by, to a day when I went down for a look in the hogpen. The hogs grunted, pointed their ears, and looked up at me with their little pig eyes close together.

There under the slop trough I saw it. The proof I was not seeking. I saw a piece of old sack. I screamed what the whole world already knew. "They threw the sack and Homer in it into the hogpen. The hogs ate up Old Homer." I leaned against the pen and I retched until I spit up. I was really sick. The hogs saw it. Bud did, too, for he was in the plum grove, spying as usual. I started running, jumped some puddles, got tired, and came to stop where some daisies covered with dust were beside the road.

I began feeling nice. The daisies were nice. Old Marth's place behind me was nice. Up overhead the fleecy sheep clouds stood stock still to become masses of daisies. Over to the left was a patch of red sky clover. Then the sheep clouds moved together and formed a maze and across the sky was a swath of daisies. Just like the swath Homer had traveled up the trace to the top of the ridge. I was delighted and looked a long while. I know I saw it. There placed in the maze of daisies he loved so well was Homer-snake. He stood upright on the end of his blunt tail and looking over the daisies, he laughed at me.

I laughed and went home.

Maw's kitchen was nice with smells of sassafras tea, spice-wood, gingerroot, milk cheeseing, and cold mint water fresh from the spring.

Bud came in the door, reporting on me. "Maw, I saw her. She has been down to Old Marth's hogpen."

"Whatever for, child?"

Maw didn't expect an answer, and I had already turned my back on Bud. I felt something new in my life. The day was coming soon when I could handle Bud. Maw refers to it as *patience*. Patience was something Bud did not have. Bud hung around, waiting on me to start talking and telling everything. I sat until Bud gave up and left, then I told Maw, "I saw Old Homer-snake among the daisies in the sky. He stood up on his blunt tail and laughed at me."

Maw left her dough-making and with flour up to her elbows, she took my head in both hands. "Precious. You saw what you hoped for, for Homer. Homer-snake is all right. You are all right. Find your little pan. You can come help me make up this bread."

Who Has Lived from
A Child with Chickens

JANET KAUFFMAN

*H*ester, Melissa, and Colleen were the three chickens who turned everything around, who ended the reign of Ratzafratz the Fat—our Razzie, our Raz—and who restored as nearly as possible the Age of Egg, with its routine perfections and disproportions in form and taste. An egg is no sphere; and this is no tale of senti-ment; it's no *Animal Farm* with sides to jump to or enemies to chuck. A sequence of events occurred. Simply. The way things do.

Queen for an episode or two was Colleen, the usual dullard; Hester and Melissa attended, dotingly. I am talking about Col-leen the Chicken, a commonplace Rhode Island Red with typical-ly underdeveloped comb. Unlike Hester and Melissa, Colleen was named for a person, a sweet-faced college freshman who sat weightlessly in a front-row seat in my General Civ class—a guileless, guiltless child who still wrote, in 1973, letters to the student paper chastising the school's cheerleaders for their slumping and scowling at games; she knew by instinct the traditional rules of conduct and experienced what appeared to be allergenic reactions to breaches of such codes. She had blue eyes, always misted as if by a mysterious makeup. Colleen the Chicken resembled Colleen the Child not at all, but when Colleen Chicken scuffed her way under the wire fence for the third time and the kids said, "Hey, let's name the one that always gets out!" I naturally said, "Why not?" It was my turn to name. Hester and Melissa were Robbie and Cy's picks, names yanked from the air. They were chickens with no heritage.

The tunneling hen didn't remind me of anybody; she was molting, still more chick than hen. I stood, stumped, at the wire fence, bending it up for the chicken to crawl back. "No name. I give up."

Robbie was five, Marine-square.

"All right," he said, "give me the first name that comes to your head."

"Colleen."

The syllables were there: wide and shining and imprecise. It felt like a reflex, a throwback, this recollection of Colleen, her wide milkface, the slightly crooked nose, her wool sweaters and long bland curls. The only time I heard her speak, she complained to a friend about the awful humidity frizzing her hair. Her voice was not unpleasant, and her hair, I decided then, was her fairest feature. So Colleen it was. And was to be. Not Joyce, the freckled, promiscuous, lyrical; not Sue, the muscled swimmer who lived like a hermit and ate only Cheezits; not Rosemary Dunlap (Dr. Dunlap) who lived upstairs on our Dorchester Street place and had screaming fits on her latticed sunporch. Colleen was the one who floated up first, a breathy balloon.

The three years that Razzie held sway in the goat shed were years of drought, tornado, and freeze. Weeds flourished and bloomed lustily while the eggplants stood stunted, skeletal, each with its four yellow leaves. Aphids ate everything decorative, including a hedgerow of hardy multiflora. A tornado lifted a trailer down the road and dropped a doorknob on our driveway. We knew it was a plague—there is always one plague or another—but we had no idea, understandably, that Razzie the Fat was implicated. At first, we (me and Hazard, my husband) worried that, as for the eggplants, our applications of mulch were to blame, that the walnut leaves mixed with the oak may not have been acid enough. Or worse, that the goat manure we spread on the north side had leached to the south in irregular patterns and we'd planted the eggplants in the barren spots. Who could tell? I reread the Eggplant entry in the *Encyclopedia of Organic Gardening*, but found no clues. As for the aphids, I knew we had ladybugs, but not enough. It takes thousands. After the first year of devastation, I'd introduced into the coldframe a few stray ladybugs we'd found trapped between windows and storm windows in the house. My plan was to breed a horde of them to help out during the July aphid ravage. The ladybugs seemed content in the coldframe, and I thought the first week I spotted some extras. Then they disappeared. We gave up on the multiflora by late August, and they stood through the fall like winter shrubs along the boundary line. Even so, we might not have suspected an unnatural, localized plague if other things hadn't happened. For instance, the jasmine thistles.

Brittle, red-flowering thistles grew in the lawn, not just in patches, but in wide, circling swaths, which sometimes changed directions overnight. Their perfume, disorienting as fog, rose from the flowers and drifted with the motions of the plants. It was impossible to walk barefoot outside. Sneakers with socks were insufficient; the thistly spines grew luxuriantly and needled through to the ankles even though the grass was new-cut. The *Field Guide to Wildflowers* included no red-flowering thistles (ours flowered every day, flat to the ground, five-petaled, blood-red). Robbie and Cy wore long pants and high shoes for those two summers, and I finally drove to S & H for a pair of heavy-duty work boots.

After meals, I sat on the porch with my nose in a cup of cold coffee, my feet propped on the metal railing, and I remembered my great-grandmother who stirred a brew of witch hazel and barks with a hand-hammered iron spoon. I remembered a painting in the Art section of *Time* magazine of a woman on a straw prairie under an umbrella, alone and content, maybe falling asleep.

Hazard had the idea he could harvest the thistle flowers and make a sweet wine, like dandelion wine. Wearing winter gloves, he filled two brown paper bags with blossoms. "Nipped in the bud," he said on his way into the house. One night, he stepped through the bedroom door, one naked half of his body after the other, a glass of red-thistle wine in each hand. "It's perfume," he said. "For you!" And he tipped one glass, like a government official, over my head. "For me!" he said. With the other glass, he doused himself. To celebrate one more disordered fact of life, we made suffocating, jasmine love at the foot end of the bed. Part of the time, we held our noses.

Still, each winter, the thistles frosted, turned black, and died like everything else. We took heart. Winter froze what it could, and that seemed appropriate. Cold we could handle. Hazard and I decided, by January, that the summer had not really been disastrous or terrifying at all. It had been cooked up.

In the shed, Ratzafratz, too, cooled off through the winter. He made himself scarce, touring his complex of tunnels under the hay and manure in the goat stalls, and continuing on through the wallboard to the chicken room of the shed, then flat along the cement-block wall where the straw was kicked up, cushy. Every three weeks on Saturday I cleaned the shed, down to the concrete, and heaped the dark forkloads of manure onto mounds that steamed west of the barn. With all of the shed doors open, Hester, Melissa, and Colleen followed me around, snapping up the small green alfalfa leaves and the spare cuts of corn. Always we watched out for Raz, who was obese and distinguishable from any other rat by his girth, and by a black mask, raccoonlike, slipped over his nose. But in spite of his weight, he was slick, very fast, and he slipped by us, while the rest of his pack was me-

thodically, unhysterically, done in. His was a life of disappear-
ances, rejuvenations, mysteries.

To clean the shed, I used a straight-pronged garden fork, not
a wispy pitchfork for those laden hauls. A garden fork is a mur-
derous tool. In essence and function, it is four primitive iron
knives. When I got a rat with that fork, I got it twice. Hester,
Melissa, and Colleen went for the eyes, and death was quick,
decisive. I'd set my S & H boot on the body, pull back the fork,
sweep the limp soul up and lift it outside, and swing wide around,
pitching it far into the burdock for the buzzards. More ecological
than D-Con pellets. No blood, no rot.

But Raz, by fishlike maneuvering and underworld trampolin-
ing, was two feet ahead of the fork, even when I stabbed four feet
ahead in the tunnel. Sometimes I'd see a tail, snapping away, or,
turning a forkful of hay, I'd see the swatchy black nose at the
disrupted end of the tunnel, just for a blink. Then he'd suck
himself back, probably turn or roll over according to incom-
prehensible rat-body law, and be safe, breathing slowly, in the
corner of the chicken room before I could pull back my arm in
javelin form to throw the fork. He could always relax, kinglike,
somewhere in his maze; longevity alone is a solid base of power.

I knew he'd done serious damage in the shed, gnawing good
wood and probably scaring the milk from Emma Peel's udder the
one night I went out and found her sitting, stricken, in the
ridiculous way goats can sit, like teen-agers with long arms dangling, not a drop of milk in her, for no reason. The rat could be
petty. Colleen, loose from her room, was beside Emma that night,
pacing, clucking a low muttering cluck. Ratzafratz may have gone
bodily through the plasterboard wall of the chicken room; I
discovered a wide tear, with six inches of chalky board crumbling
and hanging loose. Colleen could have, must have, walked right
through.

Colleen was beginning to approximate the attitudes of her
namesake, looking blandly, judgmentally at me—things were not
as they should be. Definitely not, in her eyes, as they should be.

From the night she appeared at Emma Peel's side, Colleen

assumed an authority in the shed that surprised us all, walking around in the center of things, leading Hester and Melissa down the slide in the morning, scratching up the first sow bug. In the past, she'd been a malingerer, really, sometimes just perching dreamily at the edge of the nest boxes, eating casually without any flutter, sometimes not going outside all day. She'd laid large eggs, without any of the usual fuss.

But through that last winter, she began building up a good fluff of feathers; the red skin spots she used to peck and rub open were gradually filled out with soft, small, hairlike feathers, and these then were covered, layered, with the flat red, overlapped look of healthy Rhode Island feathering. There were tufts, almost epaulets, on her shoulders, and her tail was an alert comprehen-sive fan.

By spring Hester and Melissa were shaping up, too. The three, when they walked around the bare chicken yard, picked up their feet and stepped in full-length strides. They turned in file, the inside one pivoting with real precision, the others lengthening their steps, circling around. I didn't mention their exercises to anybody; in fact, I pretended not to notice, and just looked side-long at the drills while I pinched the Japanese beetles off the Chinese elm. But one day Cy yelled from the porch, "The chickens are marching!" Thereafter their habits became a subject for family discussion, Hazard pointing out to the children that chickens were just chickens. "But, evidently," I carped back, "weather is no longer weather, nor nature, nature."

Of some interest to me, who has lived from a child with chickens, was the alteration in Colleen's comb—it was still small, as hens' combs are, but it glistened, took on a bluish cast, very much like the sudden paling, the blanching to blue, that occurs at chicken death. When a dog hits a chicken, one knows by the comb how bad it is, and if there's hope. But Colleen's comb both blued and flourished; she looked better than ever. She looked strong, like a WAC.

I was glad to see something that hinted of strength and good circulation—it hadn't rained once in April, just a light drizzle on

May Day, and the rest of May withered on, wilting. The *Almanac,* once again, was all lies. We watered the coldframe, but the seedlings were giving away moisture to air; their stems would fall flat on the sand—I could see the vermiculite lumps right through them—by late afternoon. The garden lay yellow and dry, loose as a beach, down a foot, and there it would turn into hard-pan, packed solid as boards. Our lawn never greened, although the red-petaled thistles were coming on strong.

June the first, having no garden, no grass, nothing to worry about losing, I decided to let the chickens out of their yard, to scratch at will.

Colleen stepped out first, Melissa and Hester in line behind, four and a half paces apart. With some fancy footwork, Colleen and the others surrounded the first thistle plant they came to, and, in precisely coordinated fashion, pecked it to pieces, red flowers going down last, little pompoms in beaks.

Robbie said, "Wow."

I thought, There's a plan here. Intuitive rigor. They move by design. But I said, "Yeah."

The face of Colleen the Child floated back, her brows set; she'd approve of these chickens—they figured things out with their flat circly eyes, saw a job, and got at it. It was easy to do what had to be done, and they had the gizzard to do it. Eat thistles. I felt humble, glad I'd acknowledged their talents, their taste. During the weeks of scooping cracked cornmeal into their feeder, I'd noticed with discomfort how the feed bags puffed a dry dust into my nose, and I'd thought how the chickens must suffer, the tiny holes of their beaks stuffing up, their feathers filling with dry small flakes from the kernels. I'd done the right thing finally opening their gate and giving them greenery, good juices.

That afternoon, while I was holding a hose on a three-foot pear tree, Robbie tore around the corner of the house, his whole body leaning, boots nearly sliding from under him, yelling, "Colleen's got a rat! Cornered!"

"Raz?"

"I don't know. Big as a groundhog."

"That's him!" And I was halfway around the house. "Get the fork!"

When I hit the path to the shed, I could see Colleen, her wings flung back in her most militant stance; she was side-stepping a definite half-circle in one corner of the yard, back and forth, solid and fierce, with Hester and Melissa behind her on either side, backing her up. Ratzafratz it was—in the corner, up on his hind legs, as wide as he was high, his two teeth out like an armored bib, his bent, black-wire claws stabbing ping ping ping toward Colleen, his motions stirring up heat waves out through the yard.

"Where's the fork?" I screamed at Robbie, who didn't budge at the back porch. Colleen glanced in my direction, giving me the go-ahead. I had to shrug, empty-handed. When we both looked back at Ratzafratz, he'd converted himself to empty space. The air spread out, absolutely still. A clean, perfect getaway.

She'd done more than her part, getting him out in broad daylight, out in the open yard. I was astonished at her commitment to duty, a duty beyond her realm, to my mind. If she'd scratched out a letter to Senator Plampin and complained about road crews pulling up bittersweet, endangered as it was, I wouldn't have been more impressed. Here was a blatant abuse confronted forthwith, forthright. Thoughtlessly. Colleen had no understanding of moments, of lapses. Razzie may also have turned in his mind the matter of Colleen's nerve. I'm sure he had not anticipated her moves.

That evening—as the TV predicted: it was no surprise—the weather switched: the vacant clear skies of two months were sucked eastward in a vacuumlike wind, and huge rolls of black and gray-green clouds tumbled in from the west. There were hours of dusk as the doomy underbellies of storm clouds trapped a steady, dim light. Tornado watches were posted and I knew we were in for it. By the time Hazard got home, the evening had turned into a heavy, noisy blackness, and we carried the radio and flashlights into the basement, took a pop-up book for the kids, some beers, and old blankets for the cold floor.

I felt better than usual about the animals, nature back in season as it seemed to be. I didn't worry much until one blast of wind and sledge-hammering thunder took out the electricity, and in the first pause after that blow I thought I heard Emma Peel baa her high whinnying baa. But, with a couple of hours until morning, I just shut my ears, let the house shudder, and imagined myself like Razzie, wedged in a tunnel, Colleen nearby with her dull eyes open, everything blowing over.

After a storm it's never easy to take the first look around, but this time I was upstairs in the kitchen and out the back door with the earliest light. Wind was still thumping the windowpanes roped to the coldframe and whishing hard across the back yard, whipping thistles. I could see the shed, in solid outline. Closer, slight damage—the front door, never quite straight, was pulled from one hinge, tipped out and wide open; some shingles were torn, some gone; the big window in the chicken room was cracked across. Colleen was standing in the open door, triumphant, I thought—no, shoulders back slightly, appropriately, her simple greeting.

She stepped aside according to antique protocol, then she turned and walked into the chicken room and hopped in her nest box. She was back on schedule. I walked ahead to the goat stalls, where Emma and Shy Violet blinked at me, head-on, emptily. The old diehard look. Somewhere behind a wall Melissa and Hester scratched and clucked indifferently, just as they had in bygone days, not minding Colleen.

I went back to the chicken room to check out Colleen, and I saw them, both of them: Colleen with her old-fashioned slump, squatting dreamy-eyed there in her box, egg laid, the blank calm of her life returned; and off to the side, Ratzafratz, flat on his back, already stiff, near the feeder, his claws skimpy, hooked into nothing.

I checked him over for blood, wounds—the chickens had got at his eyes, but otherwise he looked clean. "Hmmm. Colleen." I looked her in the eye, but she stared back at me from far off in chickenworld, flat-eyed, unblinking, not hiding anything. A shadow wavered across her beak—no, not a shadow, some dark hairs. I looked back at Razzie, then picked up a stiff weed out of the straw and used it to lift the hairs at his neck. Colleen would go for the jugular. She'd been through training.

The straw in that corner of the room was scruffed in a triangle, the same lines I'd seen in the chicken yard. I don't think the wind could have done it. I've never read in the *How to Raise Pullets* pamphlets anything comprehensive about chicken-scratch patterns, or tactics and attitudes of defense. Somebody should write these things down.

Predictably, after that night of storm it rained for three days, consolingly, the kind of rain that could help Ratzafratz to his colorful, chemical decay.

We buried him out on the boundary line, between two bare multiflora stalks, having determined, in council, that his was a passing worthy of ceremony.

Colleen didn't notice the funeral in the rain; it was very simple—we put him in a hole and covered him up.

This summer, as should be the case in temperate zones, the garden is growing and the redroots, naturally, are shading out carrots and celery. The ordinary scene. The daily trouble. I've no complaints. Melissa, Hester, and Colleen wiped out the thistles in the yard, and all three are molting again, as they should. I still clean the shed every three weeks, fork rats when I must.

These days of drifting July heat, I've wondered sometimes if Colleen from college ever figured a way to embrace the humid, swirling hemisphere that messed her hair. She probably still wears campus coordinates, still knows precisely what she thinks. I imagine her fierce, decorous, dull. But in these years of unaccountable catastrophe and rescue, I've learned—let's see—the generosity of fair report. And as far as Colleen goes, Chicken or Child, I simply give credit where credit is due.

One Whale, Singing

KERI HULME

*T*he ship drifted on the summer night sea.

"It is a pity," she thought, "that one must come on deck to see the stars. Perhaps a boat of glass, to see the sea streaming past, to watch the nightly splendour of stars . . ." Something small jumped from the water, away to the left. A flash of phosphorescence after the sound, and then all was quiet and starlit again.

They had passed through krillswarms all day. Large areas of the sea were reddish-brown, as though an enormous creature had wallowed ahead of the boat, streaming blood.

"Whale-feed," she had said, laughing and hugging herself at the thought of seeing whales again. "Lobster-krill," he had corrected, pedantically.

The crustaceans had swum in their frightened jerking shoals, mile upon mile of them, harried by fish that were in turn pursued and torn by larger fish.

She thought, it was probably a fish after krill that had leaped then. She sighed, stroking her belly. It was the lesser of the two evils to go below now, so he didn't have an opportunity to come on deck and suggest it was better for the coming baby's health, and hers, of course, that she came down. The cramped cabin held no attraction: all that was there was boneless talk, and one couldn't see stars, or really hear the waters moving.

Far below, deep under the keel of the ship, a humpback whale sported and fed. Occasionally, she yodelled to herself, a long un-dulating call of content. When she found a series of sounds that pleased, she repeated them, wove them into a band of har-monious pulses.

Periodically she reared to the surface, blew, and slid smooth-ly back under the sea in a wheel-like motion. Because she was pregnant, and at the tailend of the southward migration, she had no reason now to leap and display on the surface.

She was not feeding seriously; the krill was there, and she swam amongst them, forcing water through her lips with her large tongue, stranding food amongst the baleen. When her mouth was full, she swallowed. It was leisurely, lazy eating. Time enough for recovering her full weight when she reached the cold seas, and she could gorge on a ton and a half of plankton daily.

Along this coast, there was life and noise in plenty. Shallow grunting from a herd of fish, gingerly feeding on the fringes of the krill shoal. The krill themselves, a thin hiss and crackle through the water. The interminable background clicking of shrimps. At times, a wayward band of sound like bass organ-notes sang through the chatter, and to this the whale listened attentively, and sometimes replied.

The krill thinned: she tested, tasted the water. Dolphins had passed recently. She heard their brief commenting chatter, but did not spend time on it. The school swept round ahead of her, and vanished into the vibrant dark.

He had the annoying habit of reading what he'd written out loud. "We can conclusively demonstrate that to man alone belong true intelligence and self-knowledge."

He coughs.

Taps his pen against his lips. He has soft, wet lips, and the sound is a fleshy slop! slop!

She thinks:

> Man indeed! How arrogant! How ignorant!
> Woman would be as correct, but I'll settle for
> humanity. And it strikes me that the quality
> humanity stands in need of most is true in-
> telligence and self-knowledge.

"For instance, Man alone as a species, makes significant arte-facts, and transmits knowledge in permanent and durable form."

He grunts happily.

"In this lecture, I propose to . . ."

> But how do they know? she asks herself. About
> the passing on of knowledge among other species?
> They may do it in ways beyond our capacity to
> understand . . . that we are the only ones to
> make artefacts I'll grant you, but that's because
> us needy little adapts have such pathetic bodies,
> and no especial ecological niche. So hooks and
> hoes, and steel things that gouge and slay, we
> produce in plenty. And build a wasteland of
> drear ungainly hovels to shelter our vulnerable
> hides.

She remembers her glass boat, and sighs. The things one could create if one made technology servant to a humble and creative imagination . . . He's booming on, getting into full lec-tureroom style and stride.

". . . thus we will show that no other species, lacking as they do artefacts, an organized society, or even semblances of culture . . ."

> What would a whale do with an artefact, who is
> so perfectly adapted to the sea? Their conception

of culture, of civilisation, must be so alien that
we'd never recognise it, even if we were to stum-
ble on its traces daily.

She snorts.

He looks at her, eyes unglazing, and smiles.

"Criticism, my dear? Or you like that bit?"

"I was just thinking . . ."

Thinking, as for us passing on our knowledge,
hah! We rarely learn from the past or the present, and what we pass on for future humanity is
a mere jumble of momentarily true facts, and odd
snippets of surprised self-discoveries. That's not
knowledge . . .

She folds her hands over her belly. You in there, you won't
learn much. What I can teach you is limited by what we are.
Splotch goes the pen against his lips.

"You had better heat up that fortified drink, dear. We can't
have either of you wasting from lack of proper nourishment."

Unspoken haw haw haw.

Don't refer to it as a person! It is a canker in me,
a parasite. It is nothing to me. I feel it squirm and
kick, and sicken at the movement.

He says he's worried by her pale face. "You shouldn't have
gone up on deck so late. You could have slipped, or something,
and climbing tires you now, you know."

She doesn't argue any longer. The arguments follow well-
worn tracks and go in circles.

"Yes," she answers.

but I should wither without that release, that solitude, that keep away from you.

She stirs the powder into the milk and begins to mix it rhyth-
mically.

I wonder what a whale thinks of its calf? So large
a creature, so proven peaceful a beast, must be
motherly, protective, a shielding benevolence
against all wildness. It would be a sweet and

milky love, magnified and sustained by the en-
compassing purity of water . . .

A swarm of insectlike creatures, sparkling like a galaxy, each
a pulsing lightform in blue and silver and gold. The whale sang for
them, a ripple of delicate notes, spaced in a timeless curve. It
stole through the lightswarm, and the luminescence increased
brilliantly.

Deep within her, the other spark of light also grew. It was
the third calf she had borne; it delighted her still, that the swift
airy copulation should spring so opportunely to this new life. She
feeds it love and music, and her body's bounty. Already it re-
sponds to her crooning tenderness, and the dark pictures she
sends it. It absorbs both, as part of the life to come, as it nests
securely in the waters within.

She remembers the nautilids in the warm oceans to the north,
snapping at one another in a cannibalistic frenzy.

She remembers the oil-bedraggled albatross, resting with patient finality on the water-top, waiting for death.

She remembers her flight, not long past, from killer whales,
and the terrible end of the other female who had companied her
south, tongue eaten from her mouth, flukes and genitals ripped,
bleeding to a slow fought-against end.

And all the memories are part of the growing calf.

More krill appeared. She opened her mouth, and glided
through the shoal. Sudden darkness for the krill. The whale
hummed meanwhile.

He folded his papers contentedly.

"Sam was going on about his blasted dolphins the other night
dear."

"Yes?"

He laughed deprecatingly. "But it wouldn't interest you. All
dull scientific chatter, eh?"

"What was he saying about, umm, his dolphins?"

"O, insisted that his latest series of tests demonstrated their high intelligence. No, that's misquoting him, potentially high in-telligence. Of course, I brought him down to earth smartly. Results are as you make them, I said. Nobody has proved that the animals have intelligence to a degree above that of a dog. But it made me think of the rot that's setting in lately. Inspiration for this lecture indeed."

"Lilley?" she asked, still thinking of the dolphins, "Lilley dem-onstrated evidence of dolphinese."

"Lilley? That mystical crackpot? Can you imagine anyone ever duplicating his work? Hah! Nobody has, of course. It was all in the man's mind."

"Dolphins and whales are still largely unknown entities," she murmured, more to herself than to him.

"Nonsense, my sweet. They've been thoroughly studied and dissected for the last century and more." She shuddered. "Rather dumb animals, all told, and probably of bovine origin. Look at the incredibly stupid way they persist in migrating straight into the hands of whalers, year after year. If they were smart, they'd have organised an attacking force and protected themselves!"

He chuckled at the thought, and lit his pipe.

"It would be nice to communicate with another species," she said, more softly still.

"That's the trouble with you poets," he said fondly. "Dream marvels are to be found from every half-baked piece of pseudo-science that drifts around. That's not seeing the world as it is. We scientists rely on reliably ascertained facts for a true picture of the world."

She sat silently by the pot on the galley stove.

An echo from the world around, a deep throbbing from miles away. It was both message and invitation to contribute. She mused on it for minutes, absorbing, storing, correlating, winding her song meanwhile experimentally through its interstices—then dropped her voice to the lowest frequencies. She sent the message along first, and then added another strength to the cold wave that travelled after the message. An oceanaway, someone would collect the cold wave, and store it, while it coiled and built to uncontrollable strength. Then, just enough would be released to generate a superwave, a gigantic wall of water on the surface of the sea. It was a new thing the sea-people were experimenting with. A protection. In case.

She began to swim further out from the coast. The water flowed like warm silk over her flanks, an occasional interjectory current swept her, cold and bracing, a touch from the sea to the south. It became quieter, a calm freed from the fights of crabs and the bickerings of small fish. There was less noise too, from the strange turgid craft that buzzed and clattered across the ocean-ceiling, dropping down wastes that stank and sickened.

A great ocean-going shark prudently shifted course and flicked away to the side of her. It measured twenty feet from shovel-nose to crescentic tailfin, but she was twice as long and would grow a little yet. Her broad deep body was still well-fleshed and strong, in spite of the vicissitudes of the northward breeding trek: there were barnacles encrusting her fins and lips and head, but she was unhampered by other parasites. She blew a raspberry at the fleeing shark and beat her flukes against the ocean's pull in an ecstacy of strength.

"This lecture," he says, sipping his drink, "this lecture should cause quite a stir. They'll probably label it conservative, or even reactionary, but of course it isn't. It merely urges us to keep our feet on the ground, not go hunting off down worthless blind side-trails. To consolidate data we already have, not, for example, to speculate about so-called ESP phenomena. There is far too much mysticism and airy-fairy folderol in science these days. I don't wholly agree with the Victorians' attitude, that science could explain all, and very shortly would, but it's high time we got things back to a solid factual basis."

"The Russians," she says, after a long moment of non-committal silence, "the Russians have discovered a form of photography that shows all living things to be sources of a strange and beautiful energy. Lights flare from finger tips. Leaves coruscate. All is living effulgence."

He chuckles again.

"I can always tell when you're waxing poetic." Then he taps out the bowl of his pipe against the side of the bunk, and leans forward in a fatherly way.

"My dear, if they have, and that's a big if, what difference could that possibly make. Another form of energy? So what?"

"Not just another form of energy," she says somberly. "It makes for a whole new view of the world. If all things are repositories of related energy, then humanity is not alone . . ."

"Why this of solitariness, of being alone. Communication with other species, man is not alone, for God's sake! One would think you're becoming tired of us all!"

He's joking.

She is getting very tired. She speaks tiredly.

"It would mean that the things you think you are demonstrating in your paper . . ."

"Lecture."

"Work . . . those things are totally irrelevant. That we may be on the bottom of the pile, not the top. It may be that other creatures are aware of their place and purpose in the world, have no need to delve and paw a meaning out. Justify themselves. That they accept all that happens, the beautiful, the terrible, the sickening, as part of the dance, as the joy or pain of the joke. Other species may somehow be equipped to know fully and consciously what truth is, whereas we humans must struggle, must struggle blindly to the end."

He frowns, a concerned benevolent frown.

"Listen dear, has this trip been too much. Are you feeling at the end of your tether, tell us truly? I know the boat is old, and not much of a sailer, but it's the best I could do for the weekend. And I thought it would be a nice break for us, to get away from

the university and home. Has there been too much work involved? The boat's got an engine after all . . . would you like me
to start it and head back for the coast?"

She is shaking her head numbly.

He stands up and swallows what is left of his drink in one
gulp.

"It won't take a minute to start the engine, and then I'll set
that pilot thing, and we'll be back in sight of land before the morning. You'll feel happier then."

She grips the small table.

Don't scream, she tells herself, don't scream.

Diatoms of phantom light, stray single brilliances. A high
burst of dolphin sonics. The school was returning. A muted rasp
from shoalfish hurrying past. A thing that curled and coiled in a
drifting aureole of green light.

She slows, buoyant in the water.

Green light: it brings up the memories that are bone deep in
her, written in her very cells. Green light of land.

She had once gone within yards of shore, without stranding.
Curiosity had impelled her up a long narrow bay. She had edged
carefully along, until her long flippers touched the rocky bottom.
Sculling with her tail, she had slid forward a little further, and
then lifted her head out of the water. The light was bent, the
sounds that came to her were thin and distorted, but she could
see colors known only from dreams and hear a music that was
both alien and familiar.

(Christlookitthat!)

(Fuckinghellgetoutahereitscomingin)

The sound waves pooped and spattered through the air, and
things scrambled away, as she moved herself back smoothly into
deeper water.

A strange visit, but it enabled her to put images of her own
to the calling dream.

Follow the line to the hard and aching airswept land, lie upon solidity never before known until strained ribs collapse from weight of body never before felt. And then, the second beginning of joy . . .

She dreams a moment, recalling other ends, other beginnings. And because of the web that streamed between all members of her kind, she was ready for the softly insistent pulsation that wound itself into her dreaming. Mourning for a male of the species, up in the cold southern seas where the greenbellied krill swarm in unending abundance. Where the killing ships of the har pooners lurk. A barb sliced through the air in an arc and embedded itself in the lungs, so the whale blew red in his threshing agony. Another that sunk into his flesh by the heart. Long minutes later, his slow exhalation of death. Then the gathering of light from all parts of the drifting corpse. It condensed, vanished . . . streamers of sound from the dolphins who shoot past her, somersaulting in their strange joy.

The long siren call urges her south. She begins to surge upward to the sweet night air.

She says, "I must go on deck for a minute."

They had finished the quarrel, but still had not come together. He grunts, fondles his notes a last time, and rolls over in his sleeping bag, drawing the neck of it tightly close.

She says wistfully,
"Goodnight then,"
and climbs the stairs heavily up to the hatchway.

"You're slightly offskew," she says to the Southern Cross, and feels the repressed tears begin to flow down her cheeks. The stars blur.

Have I changed so much?
Or is it this interminable deadening pregnancy?
But his stolid, sullen, stupidity!
He won't see, he won't see, he won't see
anything.

She walks to the bow, and settles herself down, uncomfortably aware of her protuberant belly, and begins to croon a song of comfort to herself.

And at that moment the humpback hit the ship, smashing through her old and weakened hull, collapsing the cabin, rending timbers. A mighty chaos . . .

Somehow she found herself in the water, crying for him, swimming in a circle as though among the small debris she might find a floating sleeping bag. The stern of the ship is sinking, poised a moment dark against the stars, and then it slides silently under.

She strikes out for a shape in the water, the liferaft? The dinghy?

And the shape moves.

The humpback, full of her dreams and her song, had beat blindly upward, and was shocked by the unexpected fouling. She lies, waiting on the water-top.

The woman stays where she is, motionless except for her paddling hands. She has no fear of the whale, but thinks, "It may not know I am here, may hit me accidentally as it goes down."

She can see the whale more clearly now, an immense zeppelin shape, bigger by far than their flimsy craft had been, but it lies there, very still . . .

She hopes it hasn't been hurt by the impact, and chokes on the hope.

There is a long moaning call then, that reverberates through her. She is physically swept, shaken by an intensity of feeling, as though the whale has sensed her being and predicament, and has offered it all it can, a sorrowing compassion.

Again the whale makes the moaning noise, and the woman calls, as loudly as she can, "Thank you, thank you" knowing that it is meaningless, and probably unheard. Tears stream down her face once more.

The whale sounded so gently she didn't realise it was going at all.

"I am now alone in the dark," she thinks, and the salt water laps round her mouth. "How strange, if this is to be the summation of my life."

In her womb the child kicked. Buoyed by the sea, she feels the movement as something gentle and familiar, dear to her for the first time.

But she begins to laugh.

The sea is warm and confiding, and it is a long long way to shore.

Day After Day,
Like A Terrible Fish

DIANE McPHERSON

"**G**rab a rake, dear," Marie says when I come up the beach. She's standing up to her wader-tops in muck, feeling between her feet with one bare hand for a clam; that's why I don't get a welcoming hug. Instead I pick up a rake and go looking for a good spot, which I probably won't know when I find it.

This is just another in a long list of things that make me all wrong as her son's wife: I'm no good as a clam digger. The rest of the family is tall and athletic and extroverted. I'm shy and secretive and I hate it outdoors. It's the first weekend in December, a cold wind is coming in off the bay, and I've been lagging along the slimy beach, wishing I'd taken my down vest out of the car.

There's an art to digging clams. You take the rake, which has long curved fingers and a short handle, and you drive it straight down into the mud near the round holes the clams use for taking in sea water. Sometimes if you step near these holes you can get them to squirt, and then you know for sure you're in the right place. It takes all your strength to push the rake all the way into the mud. I have to jump on it to drive the tines in, and when I turn over a clump of mud there sometimes aren't any clams in it. Or, if I'm lucky enough to find them, they're usually impaled on the tines of the rake, which is bad, or the squirting thing turns out to be one of those long red worms with the million legs.

Albert, my father-in-law, says "Got one," when he sees me pull a crushed shell off my rake. I throw the mangled thing up the beach in disgust, but Phoebe, the fat retriever, brings it back and drops it into the hod on top of the eight other miserable clams I've turned up.

My running nose and frozen fingers finally drive me off the beach, and I make some excuse about wanting to visit with Alison. "Tell her to put some water on for tea," Marie yells after me. Alison is my sister-in-law, married to Owen's brother Simon. She's pregnant with the first grandchild and has been excused from hard labor.

While I'm blowing my nose in the bathroom I hear Alison calling me from the guest room where she and Simon sleep when they visit. I find her lying on the bed, looking pale and tired, with her shoes still on.

"Are you feeling sick?" I ask, and I start to untie her shoes for her. Alison was in my dorm in college, but she was a resident advisor when I was a freshman, so we weren't close. After she graduated we didn't stay in touch. When I married into the family three years ago, it was a surprise to both of us.

"Cramps," Alison tells me, nodding at her little round stomach. She's almost four months but there's barely a lump. "I've been spotting. I might be losing the baby."

"Should I call a doctor?" I ask, feeling panicky. I'm not too good in emergencies. If there's blood I generally faint.

"I saw my doctor yesterday before we came here," Alison says, "and he thinks there's nothing to do but wait. He's only half an hour away, if I need him. Do you have any cigarettes?"

"I thought you quit," I say, but I light one anyway, and hand it over. We're always getting lectures from Marie about the evils of smoking, and I haven't seen Alison with a cigarette since she got pregnant. I thought I was the last holdout.

"No, I just cut down," Alison says, and laughs. "I told Marie I quit to get her off my back. When we visit here I have to go for a lot of walks."

"Did you tell her about the baby?"

Alison takes a long, satisfied drag. "If you hear them coming in pretend you're smoking this," she says, and hands me the cigarette so we can share it. "Marie knows something's wrong," Alison tells me, "I told her yesterday. Simon didn't want me to come but the doctor said go ahead, and I told him I wanted to see you."

I wanted to see her, too. I used to think Alison didn't like me until a weekend she and I and Owen and Simon spent here at the farm, taking care of the animals while Owen's parents were in New Orleans. There was a blizzard, and Owen and Simon played Monopoly while Alison and I sat in the kitchen drinking wine and smoking and feeding the fire. She told me she didn't think I liked her, either, and I admitted I did resent her because she always did everything right and I didn't, and Owen's parents seemed to like her so much more than they liked me.

"They like you, Margo," Alison said. "We all do." But she knew what I meant. I don't shine in that family, and she does. Since that weekend, when we're at the farm together, Alison makes it a point to ask me in front of my in-laws how my painting is going, and if I've had any new shows. She knows I wouldn't volunteer the information.

Now I tell her, "I didn't want to come this weekend. I was going to pretend to be sick, but Owen said they were counting on us to help. I'm nervous about having them shoot the pigs."

"So am I," Alison says. "I offered to pay a man to come from the slaughterhouse to kill them, but of course Albert refused. 'If you can eat it, you can kill it' he told me. What a mule that man is!"

I like this description of my father-in-law. From the bedroom window I can see him passing the house on his way to the barn, carrying the clam hod. He's in his early sixties and built like a pack animal. His shoulders are wide and stooped, and he carries the full clam hod like it's weightless, swinging it back and forth in one hand. While he walks he looks at the ground, frowning. He's probably thinking about the work we'll be doing tomorrow, butchering the three pigs.

"We were supposed to put water on for tea," I tell Alison. "The executioner just came back from the beach."

She makes a face and takes a last grateful drag on our cigarette. "I'll pay you back," she says, "if you run out. I'll drive you to the store." After she flushes the cigarette down the john, she waves a magazine around to clear the room of smoke. I slip the rest of the pack under the comforter on the guest bed as soon as I hear the front door open. Alison is thirty-five and I'm thirty-two, but when we visit our in-laws we turn into guilty little girls. Some of it's them, I think, and some of it's us.

Marie, who is usually not sentimental, has already bought the baby a Christmas present: a kaleidoscope. This is not the kind with the pieces of plastic, but one with mirrors that make patterns out of tiny reflections of things in the room. When Marie comes in to make tea she shows it to me, saying "Look, I bought this for the baby. I couldn't resist." Then she remembers there might not be a baby yet, and her face falls, just for a second. Alison tells me "Look through it, Margo. We've been using it all weekend. I couldn't wait to see what you'd think of it."

When I hold it to my eye, I see what she means. The kaleidoscope makes all the ordinary colors in the room seem to glow. They fracture like those little pieces of plastic and form gorgeous patterns I immediately think about painting, and I guess that's why Alison thought I'd like it. The spider plant hanging at a window becomes a green lattice with a lacy star at the center, and everything else around the room, azalea plant, striped chair throw, narrow-planked wood floor, makes intricate geometric patterns so lovely I keep taking the kaleidoscope away from my eye to see what might be making the colors. The room is trans-formed; it's broken down into the pieces, ordinarily not noticed, of which it's made up. Once I put the kaleidoscope down and I see that Marie and Alison have been watching me. They're smil-ing, as if I'm the child they'd bought the toy for. Have I seemed that happy with it?

By the time we finish our tea it's getting dark, feeding time. I follow Marie to the barn with a bucket of potato peels and kitch-en scraps for the pigs. It's the prisoners' last meal; they'll be shot in the morning and we'll have to do all the butchering and wrap-ping. It looks like they suspect something, too, although I know they don't have any idea it's their last day. They're standing in a gloomy line just inside their electric fence, watching us feed the chickens.

"What's wrong with these hens?" I ask Marie. The chickens are all in the fenced-in yard outside their little shed, scratching in the gravel and giving us the eye. Their back ends and heads are red and splotchy and nearly bare of feathers, and some of them have open sores. The tops of their beaks have been trimmed back so they all look like they have underbites.

"Cannibalism," Marie says, and she dumps their grain in the trough. "They eat each other. The vet says that sometimes hap-pens when the days get shorter and they're confined to their coop. He told us to trim the beaks so they can't hurt each other, and get them a radio to distract them."

I go inside the coop to collect the eggs and it's like some kind of crazy disco in there. There's a red light over the small door the chickens use to get in and out. They're listening to Pat Benatar. "Gonna use my arms, gonna use my legs," she's singing, and when they see me open the door to collect the eggs the beakless laying hens start making a loud clamor that sounds like they're singing along, "gonna use my, my, my imagination."

"Poor things," I say to Marie, "they look so ugly." I can imagine them moping on their nests all night under the red light, singing along to Top 40.

Marie laughs at me. "Lucky they can't see themselves," she says.

Next we feed the sheep and lambs, my favorites. They're all wearing little blue overcoats made from burlap, to keep their fleeces clean for spinning. The spring lambs come right up to the gate and eat hay out of my hands, but their mothers keep to the back of the fold and stare at me, giving sudden rude comments that make me jump. One of them turns her back and pees. Under the flipped-up skirt of her overcoat her vulva, bare and pink and exposed, looks like part of a woman instead of an animal. Virgin wool; it reminds me of a joke I've heard about cowboys and sheep.

The pigs are waiting for their dinner along the single strand of fencing wire that outlines their yard. They've torn up every inch of ground around their little shed, mashing it into muck, and now they're up to their knees in it, staring at us with tiny reddened eyes. The wire looks too flimsy to contain them, but it isn't. Owen and I were here for a weekend when the pigs went into their yard for the first time. They were like little naked puppies, curious and gentle; they ate out of our hands and followed us around the barn. Marie took them into the yard while Albert turned on the fence, and then we all stood around waiting for them to try to walk out. We weren't sure the fence would contain them. For a while they didn't move, but finally the most affectionate and greedy pig, later named Albert Junior, came trotting toward us and hit the fence right at the level of his flat little nose. Go back, I was thinking. Don't do it. But he just kept coming, with his little bright eyes on us. It took him all night to catch on that the fence was there. Every once in a while I'd be jolted out of sleep by the ungodly screaming of a baby pig, but after that night, they stopped trying to escape. Now the fence only comes to their knees and they could easily step over it, but they never do. They stand at their trough and wait for dinner, and attack their slop with vulgar smacking noises, sticking their heads under the stream from the bucket and letting food run down their stiff, whiskery cheeks. I know this is silly, but they look at us like they hate us.

After Marie goes back to the house I collect some windfall apples and throw them one by one into the pigpen. The pigs dive for them, landing on their knees and coming up crunching, with mud dripping from their flat snouts. It's eerie, I think, feeding something I'll soon be eating. The pigs are rude, waiting for me to throw another apple, staring without blinking, making little guttural comments to each other about me, and then defecating.

I don't feel like going back into the house right away, so I sit in the cold metal rocker on the porch, rocking and smoking, shivering from the cold metal seat. I'm wishing Owen would come out looking for me. I think he will eventually, come out in his blue parka and wrap his arms around me to warm me up; but now I can hear him laughing with his brother in the house, goofing around. They like each other but don't get together very often. They're doing a lot of thumping, and it sounds like they're playing Nerf basketball. Before her sons come to visit, Marie gets out the games and toys, as if they were still kids instead of men in their thirties. Maybe it's to remind them that they're still her children, and maybe it's to remind herself. But it's unnerving to watch Owen and Simon playing with toys on the floor in front of the hearth, with their big feet stretching halfway out into the room.

Alison comes out, pretending to be looking for me, but really so she can hide in a corner and smoke part of my cigarette. She inhales as if her life depends on it.

"How do you feel?" I ask her. I can't tell how she looks. She's in the darkest corner of the porch so I can't see her face, and she's wearing her coat and bedroom slippers.

"Fine," she says. She takes a big drag and snorts air out her nose. "You've been outside a long time."

"I know," I say, and shiver. I don't need to explain why. The big thermometer on the side of the house says 28; I can't feel my toes. "Did anyone notice?" I ask.

"I don't think so," Alison says. "They're planning the execution. It's scheduled for seven-thirty tomorrow morning."

"God," I groan, "will we all have to attend?"

"I've already refused on account of my condition," Alison says. "I can tell them I need you to hold my hand if you want to get out of it too. I don't think they'd expect us to be out there anyway, except I think Marie wants to."

"She does?" I say, like I can't believe it. But I do.

"She *says* she does, but I think she's trying to shame the boys. She told them, 'If you can eat it, you can kill it.' Simon will shit his pants when that gun goes off."

"God, they're just alike," I say, and laugh. I'm thinking no one is going to like it much, even Owen's parents, who run their farm with a merciless scientific fervor. I know it's harder to kill than it looks, because I grew up on a farm myself, my grandparents' dairy farm. I can remember my grandfather delivering calves in the middle of the night and killing a chicken for dinner. But he couldn't stand killing the big animals. He'd truck them to the slaughterhouse with a face as long as Thursday, and my grandmother and I would sit around all day feeling like we were in mourning, waiting for him to come back.

"Which pig gets it first?" I ask Alison. "Merle, or Betty, or little Albert Junior?"

Alison snorts, and a white billow of smoke comes out of her mouth and floods across the gloom we're sitting in. Some of it is smoke, and some of it is her breath in the cold air. I can see the outline of her shoulders, and a pale slice of the side of her face, and behind her the moon, a fat dumpling floating and bobbing on the sea.

"I didn't plan to have this baby," Alison says suddenly. "It was an accident. Simon talked me into keeping it. You should know that."

"Oh," I say. So that's the way it is, an accident. "How does he feel about you maybe losing it?"

"No problem," Alison says. This is Simon's favorite expression, and she says it with the same drawling inflection he uses. "We'll just start over again." This, too, sounds like Simon's expression, but I can't quite tell what she's thinking, and I can't think of anything else to say, so I ask her, "How does it feel, being pregnant?"

"Awful," she says, "I'm sick all the time. All I think about is eating, but when I eat I throw up. And now I can feel the baby thrashing around in there sometimes. You know what that feels like?"

"What?" I ask her.

"Like a fish," she says. She grinds out her cigarette and stands up to go inside. "Like a fish on a hook."

When both boys are visiting the farm at the same time, there are standard sleeping arrangements: Simon and Alison get the guest room, which used to be their room when they were first married. They're the oldest and they were married first. Owen and I get a corner of the basement. It isn't as bad as it sounds. There's a small woodstove for heat and the corner is carpeted. It has a dresser and reading lamps on tables. The sheets always feel damp, though. And when I forget to turn on the electric blanket until I go to bed (usually earlier than the rest of the family), I put on my flannel nightgown and lie shivering with my knees pulled up against me. Then I fall asleep with the blanket set all the way at ten, and wake up too hot in the middle of the night. Or, like tonight, when I'm not tired but need to be alone, I lie listening to the ceiling creak when people walk around overhead, and the water gurgles in the pipes beside me from the dishwasher. The clams we had for dinner haven't settled well, or maybe it was the dessert. My stomach is gurgling and bubbling and my legs and feet are cold. Phoebe sneaks down the stairs and thumps herself down on the carpet and sighs, and I read old copies of *The New Yorker* and wait for Owen to come to bed.

"What's up?" he asks me. He's surprised to find me still awake. I seem to sleep a lot when we visit his parents; sometimes it's tiring just talking to them. This makes Owen mad, because he can't understand why I don't think of it as my home.

"I couldn't sleep," I tell him, and slide my feet to his side of the bed. "Will you rub my feet?"

He rubs with one hand and pets the dog with the other; I can hear his hand thumping down on her head through the mattress.

"I'm worried about Alison," I tell him.

"I thought you were," he says, patting my feet under the covers, *thump-thump-thump*. "These things happen sometimes. Simon told me they were going to try again, if they lose this one."

I lift my head and look at him. "Does Alison want to try again?"

Owen shrugs. "I doubt she does right now, but Simon will change her mind. He really wants to have children." He puts one hand against my cold fanny. "God, I think you've died."

"Owen, I don't think I want to have a baby ever," I tell him. He sits back with his head on his pillow, leaned against the head of the bed. Down across his forehead and nose, and up into his hair, the lamplight draws a thin silver line that perfectly outlines his profile. If I had a piece of black paper I could trace that line and make a silhouette.

"You will someday," Owen tells me. He sounds like he's talking to the dog, or to a reluctant child, *thump-thump-thump-*, go to sleep now. He starts rubbing my feet again; through the blankets I can hear the dry sounds of his hands on my cold skin. "You don't need to start worrying about that until I've finished school, and we own a house. Then we can afford kids. A long, long time from now." He's very sure of what he's telling me. That's how all of Owen's family sounds, sure of things, sure nothing will ever go wrong. They have a plan, they stick to it. You meet someone, you see her for a while, and then as long as you seem to get along you start thinking about weddings. After a decent interval the subject of children comes up. And everyone just assumes this is the way you want it, no one asks you. No one wants to think that maybe you aren't so sure you want children at all, like Alison. Or that you're shy, like me. Introverted; afraid of just about everything new, including marriage and babies.

◆

In the morning I manage not to hear the first shot because I'm in the shower. When I come into the kitchen, rubbing my hair in a towel, Alison is in the rocking chair by the stove, and her face is the color of an eggshell.

"Are you all right?" I ask her.

She nods. "About the same. Can you see what they're doing out there? I didn't dare look."

All I can see is people standing around in the muck, looking at the pig house. "Not much going on," I tell Alison.

"I heard one shot and I felt like I was going to faint," she says, and she drops her cigarette into the top of the woodstove and immediately lights another one. She's wrapped in an army blanket, which makes her look like an invalid.

"Are you in any pain?"

"A little," she says, and shrugs. "I'm mostly cold. I'm bleeding more. I don't think it's going to stop," she says, and looks at me. She looks all right, just pale. I've never noticed before the little moustache of dark hair Alison has on her upper lip. Now it's wet from perspiration, either from a cold sweat or because she's sitting so close to the fire that I can smell the hot wool of the army blanket.

"Will you need to go to the hospital?"

"Just to the doctor's office. He said if I didn't need a D and C, he'd just examine me and send me home."

There's some thumping just outside the door. I look at Alison to see if she wants me to take the cigarette, but she just inhales and blows the smoke toward the fire.

Marie comes in the door and looks at the smoke. "Oh," she says to Alison, and she sounds forlorn, "I had such hopes of finally having a grandchild." Her boots and pantslegs are spattered with pig blood. I can smell it from where I'm sitting, and I light a cigarette myself.

In a few minutes we hear a shot from outside; Marie goes back to help. We don't want to look, but we take turns going to the kitchen window that has the best view of the pigpen. We can see the shot pig, which they've tied with two ropes; there's a big dark spot at the side of its head and it's kicking wildly, jumping against the ropes. Albert is beside it with a knife, kneeling in the mud, trying to hold it still so he can cut its throat. Simon and Owen are pulling back on the ropes. Owen's face has the same grim expression he has when he's angry with me and he's storm-ing around the house, cleaning or doing the dishes or some other chores he thinks I should have taken care of.

"Oh Jesus," Alison says, "I'm glad I don't have to be out there."

But it doesn't bother me as much as I thought it would. Some-thing about the scene reminds me of a cowboy movie; maybe it's the ropes, and the way Owen and Simon have dug their heels in-to the mud to hold back the bucking pig while it thrashes and dies. It looks exciting and inefficient, like a rodeo, and maybe that's why I can stand at the window and watch them shoot the last pig, Albert Junior. He's the smallest, but he fights harder, dragging Owen and Simon nearly to the fence before he falls to his knees in the mucky yard.

Albert has erected a big wooden scaffolding in the yard just outside the electric fence, with three nooses on it for the three carcasses. Last night he speculated that the smallest pig weighed about two hundred pounds; it takes all three men to hoist the bodies up there, where they dangle by their trotters until they're bled out. It's very cold. Steam rises from the three bodies up past the timbers, and disappears into the pale December sky. The four people I can see through the window, standing around the gal-lows, look somber, like witnesses at a hanging. They're having the obligatory moment of silence before they scald and scrape the carcasses.

After this they carry two picnic tables onto the porch, where there's some shelter from the cold sea wind. Marie lines the tables with brown paper and arranges the tools: saws and cleav-ers and long-bladed steel knives with grey worn edges. Last night I sat in the rocker by the fireplace watching Albert sharpen the knives, and his face had the same look of preoccupation I've often seen on Owen's. The knife blades flashed in the firelight across the sharpening stone with a rasping noise, *quiiiick-quiiiick,* like the sound boys make when they gather saliva into their mouths before they spit. Albert has huge hands, all scarred and knotted from hard work. He picked up knife after knife, inspecting the edges, feeling along the curves with his broad flat thumb, like someone planning a ritual murder. Then he took his pistol out of its leather case and cleaned and oiled it, and sighted down the barrel into the fire. Alison was reading; Owen and Simon were playing Monopoly, moving the tiny silver shoe and the little flat-iron with hands that were as large as their father's. Marie was knitting a baby sweater; her needles made a regular clicking sound I could hear across the room.

We go out onto the porch to see what's happening. They have the first pig on the table, and I watch them sawing off the head; the saw makes a high rasping sound on the way through the spine, the kind of sound that makes you cringe, like fingernails on slate. The body is pale, bled out, it doesn't look like something living any longer. It looks like meat.

Albert has a book about butchering, and he marks the cuts with a special pen. It's all very scientific, but the sawing noise makes me sick. And I don't like watching my husband hacking away grimly, with his jeans spattered with blood and his hands coated with fat and gobs and clots of flesh. Beside him the first severed head rests on the table, looking out to sea with its calm little eyes which I would like to close. I go back inside so I don't have to watch all those cold fingers fumbling around in the slippery layers of pigfat.

Marie brings in trays of cuts and plops them into separate piles on the counters. Alison and I are in charge of trimming and wrapping, and sawing off the ends of sharp bones. We put the excess fat in a huge kettle on the woodstove, where it slowly renders into lard. Marie tells us what each cut is but I have trouble keeping them straight. Sometimes when I have something wrapped I have to unwrap it again because I can't remember what it is. We write the names of the cuts on butcher paper with wax crayons, but when the slime from our fingers gets on the paper the crayons won't write and the tape won't hold the packages together.

Marie makes one pile of scraps which we are supposed to make into pork roasts by rolling the pieces together and tying them tight with string. Alison's roasts look like something I've seen in a butcher shop; each one has a neat layer of fat around the outside like frosting. She's sitting on a kitchen stool, pale but cheerful. She has the right attitude, she knows we're essential to the butchering process. But I can't understand how she does her work so well, how she gets her packages to look uniform and to stay shut when she tapes them. I'm having trouble with mine. All the counters are coated with a slick layer of fat that shines in the weak sunlight. We all have little nicks on our hands from the trimming knives, and from the little ragged ends of bones.

Alison comes and goes to the bathroom. I finally have to stop asking her how she's feeling every time she comes back, because the answer is always the same, she's just fine. And I can't decide if the fine means she's losing the baby, or she's not, or which I wish it would be. When I use the bathroom I'm surprised at how neat it is, no slimy fingerprints and not a trace of blood, and the towels lined neatly along the racks. I hate to go back to the kitch- en. Meat is piling up on the counters, and the packaging is getting ahead of us. Marie can't find space on the counters to put the stuff down, so she stays to help out for a while and Alison takes a rest.

When Simon comes in to warm his hands, Alison has her feet up on the fender of the woodstove, and she's just lighting a cigarette. He holds his hands flat out over the stove and looks down at her, and I watch her shake her head, No, not yet. Noth- ing's happened. Simon's fingers, pale and thick and swollen with the cold, look like bundles of sausages. He sways back and forth beside the stove, getting warm.

I can't get my packages to stay closed. I pull hard on the tape, I stretch it over the paper, but it keeps popping back off. I'm wondering if Alison was the person I heard last night, walking back and forth. I can see her in the dark corner beside the stove.

She has long brown hair which she wears pulled back in a braid, and she's wearing a navy blue sweater. Between the two darks her pale round face hangs like the moon, calm and resigned. Simon turns away from the stove and grins at me and goes back to work, turning the doorknob with his elbow to avoid touching it with his greasy hands.

After he leaves, Alison hurries to the bathroom and she's gone for a long while. I listen for something, but there's no noise; I don't know if I should go back and check on her, or stay and wrap. When she finally comes back I'm still working on the same roast. It won't stay together even though I've wound yards of string around it until it looks like it's been captured in a net.

"I guess I need to go see the doctor," Alison says. Then she looks at my face. "You better sit down, Margo. You look worse than I do."

I do feel dizzy, like someone just pulled my plug. And Alison looks fine, no worse than she has looked all day; I'm taking this worse than she is. I look around, but all of the chairs are covered with white packages that say Pork Roast, 3 lbs.; Pork Chops, 2 lbs.; Pork Tenderloin. "There isn't any place to sit," I tell her, and then I push back my hair, but I've forgotten my hands are covered with grease. They don't feel like part of me when they touch my face. They feel horrible and cold, corpse hands.

Alison talks me into going to the guest room to rest for a few minutes. It's quiet and pleasantly warm there with the sun coming in the windows, not like the damp cold cellar. I wipe the slime off my hands and face with a washcloth, but I don't dare lie down. My hair feels greasy and stuck together. I wish Owen could come in and talk to me, but he's still working, probably clenching his teeth and looking gaunt because he hasn't eaten all morning. He hates this work too, but he'll do it until he drops. I'm the only one who can't take it.

On the wall is a ragged pool of light, the reflection of a mirror on the dresser. A pale yellow spider is walking in and out of it; in the brightest spots it almost disappears. I hear people in the kitchen, but I can't make out what they're saying. My mother-in-law's voice goes up and up, asking questions, and one of the boys answers, in a voice like his father's but with his mother's inflections. Are they talking about Alison's baby, or are they talking about me?

I look at myself in the mirror; my hair is stringy and tangled, stuck together at the sides. I can't stand it that way. I carry the mirror over near the window so I can see it better, and lay it flat on the bed. When I look down into it my face looks anxiously back at me. It's like the game I liked to play as a child in my grandparents' house. Their ceilings were made of particle board with moldings along the joints that divided each ceiling into rectangles. I liked putting my grandmother's mirror on the table and looking at the ceiling that way, because when I looked down, it was like the room had flipped over and I could walk on the ceiling, stepping over moldings and walking into the neat bare rectangular chambers. It feels like I can do this now.

I try to wipe the grease off my hair with tissues. The hair gums together into a stiff mass which won't comb out, so I get Alison's sewing scissors from the dresser to trim away the worst of it. I'm only thinking of cutting away a little hair, just at the sides where it's stuck together. Then I can comb the top hair over the shorter layers. But I cut too much. A whole chunk of hair comes off and falls down. I see it falling up in the mirror, toward my face, and then the reflection meets the real hair and covers my cheek when it lands. There's a big patch of short hair, just in front of my ear. It can't be covered up, so I cut the other side. I look like one of those children's games where you make hair on the bald man by pulling iron filings around with a magnet. I cut more, lifting the hair up away from my face and cutting just above my fingers to get it even, like I remember my grandmother doing. Long curls fall down like seaweed onto the mirror. I cut by feel until the long hair is gone, and then I brush away the tangle of curls and take a look.

It's not bad. Under the shorn curls, my face is bare and round and pale, with dark sad eyes, the way it looked when I was a child. I look like a lamb, like a poor lost lamb.

In Praise of
Creeping Things

CATHY COCKRELL

W hen my mother's knitting needles made their angry clicks, when the reading light above my father, stiff in his chair, trained a yellow beam onto his page, I stood at my parents' second story window and watched the tent caterpillars spinning their white net. High in the branches of the trees that formed a screen against the neighbors, the nest was visible to me from the window, but difficult to spot from the ground below.

So when my father walked the lawn, setting up sprinklers to move and stop like clockwork, he never saw the nest until I told him where to look. It was then that he went after the caterpillars. It was then that I monitored his handiwork from above: the clippers opening at the end of the pole, severing the web; the white tent falling to the ground; the waiting can of gasoline he dunked it in; the gold flames jumping as he set the nest on fire.

After the caterpillars were wiped out, my father went hunting. For deer? For fowl? Don't be a ninny. Father hunted the back yard for moles. He examined their dirt mounds, figured possible maps of their tunnels below; he took his time. He bought mole bombs at a gardening store. He set the sticks in the mouths of the tunnels. He lit the fuses. The rest was up to your imagination: the frantic mole fleeing as the fumes surged toward it, then lying down defeated in its tomb.

Mother preferred elbow grease and offensive measures to bombs and gas after the fact. She scanned the territory out by the walk and mailbox and under the branches of the tall birches that the landscaper had ordered. She wore high rubber boots and a heavy sweater. She watched the hairline of the grass where the moles' humped grey backs first broke through the crust, before they'd made their damnable heaps in the front yard, facing the street. She walked pitchfork in hand, observant. It revolted her but it had to be done, she said, glancing toward the street, her voice thin and unconvinced. Still, she stabbed deep into their bodies, she stopped them cold.

And I was the distressed creature watching, running to the front yard, the back, comparing the successes and satisfactions of their methods, judging mother and father by their separate, self-chosen means.

Which was better? I can't answer that. Don't ask me to measure muscle against ingenuity, like dogs against cats. I can say something, though, about this: why mother would have preferred her means, father his; why mother would prefer the work of heart, adrenalin, lungs and arms, and the undeniable guilt as she stabbed clear through to the fuzzy creature's heart—she whose life seemed always separate, vague and lost. While father, after so many daily bothers at the company, could figure, set the bombs, and have it be far away down deep where the mole actually passed out in its blanket of gas and died.

My parents—no green thumbs, I might mention—were trying to keep the yard nice. They were giving a lot of parties that were important to my father's career and the subject of much tension and loud arguments. The house had to be clean; the place settings, the menu, and the yard had to be just right. Molehills were undesirable, and the leavings of stray dogs. This was before the leash laws, at a time when dogs still ran loose through the neighborhood at night leaving piles on lawns, baying, rooting in garbage cans, eating food off porch steps as the guests inside the houses simmered down into after-dinner drinks and dirty jokes not intended for the ears of children.

I can see my mother, lingering in the living room among the laughers, or coming into the kitchen where I eavesdropped, her arms weighed down with serving dishes like she was a heavyladen coat stand. She meant to set them down somewhere among the vast clutter that already filled the counters, as it did at every party, and only at parties. I picture her confused eyes and small scowl as she moved unfamiliarly in the usually immaculate room, searching for a place to put the meat platter, the vegetable dish, and the rest of her delicately balanced objects.

"Come help me," I remember her saying once, overwhelmed. "Don't just stand there. Sometimes I really can't stand you—or him!—or anyone. You're all beasts." I helped her, and as soon as all the dishes were on the counter she said, "Finish making that milkshake and run along." They hadn't meant to have me. But once I'd come nonetheless they made the best of me; I had my assets.

One of my assets was that I could climb like a tiny monkey. I hoisted myself up onto the counter to reach the shelf with the chocolate sauce while mother fussed below with the dripping serving spoons. From up there I was high enough to look out the window. I saw Bender, the fat, aged bulldog owned by the Chamblisses next door as he gobbled the first of three perfect golden-crusted dessert pies mother had set out there to cool.

I couldn't quite make out in the near darkness, but could imagine, his jowls red with the luscious raspberry meat and seeds. It came as a surprise to me, who had never known a dog and had no idea they could go for fruits and sweets.

I have to own, though, that yes, I certainly did see the bulldog's deed, and in time to have saved the day had I alarmed mother. But something about it caught me unawares and fascinated me. I mean the lights at the end of the walk shined cheerily; the dinner guests' cars were parked at the curb like docile, obedient cows; and the guests themselves were snickering, father among them, in the front room vacuumed and dusted and straightened up for the occasion—while Bender gobbled at the delicacies.

What did mother do when she went to the porch for the pies that would crown a perfect meal? Naturally she looked stunned and called father in. She told him in a loud whisper. She showed him the sweet red mess on the top cement step. Then I watched her go back into that party room. And I saw, from my low vantage point near the doorway, the little place where her smile curdled at the corner as she apologized in a way that made all the guests laugh.

I swear, though, I don't remember which came first—hating Bender or him ruining the pies, if it was before or after that that we came to curse the ways of "man's best friend." I don't remember when it was we started the mortal crusade against the Chambliss dog, hating the very thought of his mouth, shiny black and dripping. The human creature is easily molded by what's around her, and as a child, I must admit, I did my best to make "Bender" a household word of hate. I got mileage out of reporting his every trespass against the premises—not immediately, always, but eventually. Even when I needn't have, when I half hated myself for doing it, so that I felt the need to make it up to Bender, later, when we finally got acquainted.

It was I, for instance, who knew and told why the decorative evergreens died. They were low-growing pines, their roots bound in gunny sacks, that father brought home from the nursery and set down like punctuation marks at the corners of the house. Yet it's dogs, they say, who "mark" their territory. So why not come right out with it? All right, father was marking the corners of his house with shrubs, like little low parapets.

This I knew, somehow, and so appreciated Bender's brashness those autumn mornings when I saw him move along through the fog that encased and hid him, like a huge, corpulent caterpillar inside its web. He moved through the yard, careful and curious, sniffing at the edge where the grass stopped and the curved planting areas strewn with cedar bark began, at the empty air above the window well, at the smell of pebbles and tiny green weeds that grew down there.

I followed inside the house, moving from window to window to keep him in view. I watched him as he reached the azalea bushes and snarfled at their bright fallen flowers that had slid away from the pistils like a glove from a hand. Then he sniffed at the low lamps that lighted the walk, and at the three mushrooms I knew had come up through the cedar chips intended to discourage weeds, and then at the startling bursts of upright pine needles like those painted on Japanese screens.

And in spite of all the nasty things I'd ever said or heard against Bender's rolls of fat, I saw him lift his leg delicately to piss on the pine. Not only one day but twice or seven times, twenty or twenty-seven, till the thing turned piss yellow and withered up and died. I tattled, and my parents began using slingshots and BBs on Bender and the others when the neighbors weren't around.

The Chamblisses, especially, were in their front yard a lot. Mrs. knitted baby clothes in a lawn chair while Mr. worked the flower beds. They were childless people. She had been pregnant with a baby at least three times that I'd heard of, and once she got pretty far along, but every one of her babies came out dead.

"But then they finally succeeded," father cracked one day. "She had a deformed one with extra legs." He was talking about old Bender, someone else's reject that they had brought home one day from the pound. The Chamblisses were indulgent parents. For his frequent walks, they dressed Bender in a wool coat Mrs. had knitted, and they let him bay in the back yard all night long. "Like the Hound of the Baskervilles," father said, imitating Bender.

My parents liked this joke about the neighbors' mongrel offspring. When the Chamblisses passed, with Bender on a leash, mom would say, "would you look at that! I think Bender's going to have a sibling!" Then they'd peer through the window trying to decide if Mrs. Chambliss was pregnant with a second four-legged child or if they were being misled by her coat.

Mrs. Chambliss never ended up with a human child. I always imagined that made her sad, so I was surprised at how cheerful she seemed the first time I really looked at her, the day she approached me at the mailboxes. She wanted to know, would I be interested in taking care of their dog Bender while they went away on a trip? They would pay me, she promised, and the idea of earning my own money for once convinced me, even though I had always known Bender as that fat slug of a dog next door with slime dripping from every end, and even though mother and father would hate for me to get involved. They cracked a few jokes, but they let me.

It wasn't hard, either. The Chamblisses had Bender on a long chain attached to his doghouse. All I had to do was squeeze through the hedge where the stems stood wide apart, fill his bowl with chunks of hard brown food they had set in a dry place under the eaves, make sure he had fresh water, and move his piles off the lawn.

The first night I did it right after my own dinner. I remember it like yesterday because of how my father teased when I came home. He said he'd watched me across the hedge lifting Bender's piles so tenderly, like fragile fresh-baked pastries, off the Chamblisses' lawn between a pair of sticks. He'd seen old Bender come oozing up to me on the end of his chain, he told mother, laughing, and startle me so that I stuck my arm out straight and awkward to touch his neck and his rolls of fat. Dropping the pile, he told mother, right on my foot. Mother laughed a shrill, scaredish kind of laugh as I looked down, shame-faced, blushing, at the faint stain still left on my tennis shoe.

After that I only went over when the sky had turned blue-black and the first stars were stuck up there as sweet in the firmament as Bender the bulldog seemed, for all his slime and bad habits, lying there by his shed. I talked to him while I poured his food, the chunks clinking against the side of the bowl in the dark.

And I talked while the food disappeared with sharp pulverizing sounds in his jaw. Then he rubbed up against me with his pushed-in face like a shovel had whacked him. And I confessed all the terrible names I'd called him, and my part in causing the sling-shot assaults launched against him, now, whenever they saw him approach our yard.

It is mysterious, I could almost say sublime, how he seemed to forgive me. He didn't snarl or snap, nor once crow with vengeance, so to speak, as I picked up his piles with sticks to remove them. Instead he cuddled up with his appreciative wet nose and well-meaning, down-turned, drooling mouth. Which was more, I felt, than my mother would do if I messed up her kitchen; it was more than father had done when I threw off the timing on his sprinklers. And those sins of mine seemed like tiny specks compared to the malice I had harbored against the dog.

I'd go home to bed and think about it. Hunched up under the covers, I alternately embraced and fought off a new feeling about Bender that I felt sure would cause me troubles the next time they brought out the slingshot or cursed his name. Sometimes I listened to the house creak, or watched light move across my curtains from some auction or sale being advertised with big search-beams that swept across the sky like the wail of Bender that rose up for the vacationing, absent Chamblisses, or for me, maybe, maybe for me.

In the mornings father and mother, looking tired, would say it was getting worse. They didn't say what "it" was, but I knew. It was Bender. They said his baying caused them hard times "making nookie," and insomnia. Father said the racket was enough to make his hair fall out.

"They ought to put him out of his misery," father said. Mother said, beside herself: "I could strangle him." They fantasized plots against his life—standard stuff, stuff I didn't listen to but went to school and did my chores: dusted furniture, salted slugs, watched for stray dogs, fed Bender and talked to him.

The last night before the Chamblisses came home there was a light wind, no moon, and Bender began to bay. This time he really did bay deep into the night—at the no-moon, the wind, for me, for the Chamblisses, for the souls of bombed moles and the ruined splendors of tent caterpillar civilizations. For whoever and whatever a dog finds to bay about. A few hours before dawn he finally cut it out, probably tired out and deep asleep, because there wasn't another bay or bark out of him in the remaining hours of darkness or the next day, or that night, when I saw the Chamblisses' car coming back into their drive.

Awhile later they went out to feed Bender and greet him. Then the baying started up. It was the Chamblisses, though, not Bender, wailing away across the hedge. It was Mr. Chambliss with his flashlight, and the two of them dragging Bender's fat white body, like a belly-up dead slug, into the back porch light. Old Bender had died away the last night he was under my care. I was afraid they might think it was my fault—but Bender was so old, they told me, choked up, they hadn't thought he was long for this world, anyway. So I guess for them, after the first shock of it, maybe it wasn't so horrible.

But I took it hard. I didn't have a pet turtle or jumping bean, even, to make up for this hound I had watched and fed and talked to. And I wanted to find out just how Bender had died. I figured if it was by suffocating or poisoning that would tell me a thing or two. I sucked in my breath and curled into a ball like a potato bug and prayed for all the creeping things.

And from then on I have never betrayed them nor presumed to end their misery so long as it was no worse than my own. And I began to sing their praises.

Roxie Raccoon

SALLY MILLER GEARHART

"*T*here lies Lekka by the rounded stump! I, Ta, have named her and she is Shy no more!"

"Found, Lekka, found! Ta finds you and we all see you now!"

"Lekka, the white covered log—"

Circles of laughter in a cold long ago woods. Girlchildren's voices discovering Lekka, no longer deceived by her carefully-woven Shy-veil. Immersed in the memory, Ta smiled to herself. Lekka, trudging just behind her was smiling, too.

"But you're wrong," Lekka shortstretched. "That day Nita wasn't with us. And neither was Erika."

"Oh yes she was. Erika, I mean. She was just learning to Go Shy and was training on her chameleon passes. She fooled us all being that cave opening by the rock."

"Was that that day?" Lekka puzzled.

"Sure, love. And you were the log. Ah yes, you were always so good at Shy practice in the snow."

"Best place for Shy practice," Lekka was humming as she followed Ta through the showers of whiteness dropped by fir boughs.

"Right," Ta sent. "Particularly when you're so pale to start with." She ducked behind a tree to sidestep Lekka's snowball.

Lekka declined to throw another. She dusted the powder from her gloves. "O, Great Dark Ta! Truth-to-tell: didn't we always give you a handicap when we were practicing in snow? Didn't we?" She hugged Ta from behind, dragging her back to the path they were blazing in the whiteness of the hillside.

Ta grinned. She took the sweepspan now and reached out protectively beyond them both to the south, to the east and southwest. Lekka fell in behind her, playing an old game of placing her slightly smaller boots precisely in the middle of the other woman's vacated footsteps. Another white forest in another year.

Ta and Lekka were veteran Shyers now, both of them accomplished in the fade-and-focus process of blending into and separating from the textures and colors of their environment. They could speed their body-flutters to the point of invisibility and sink into rocks, trees, water, and—they hoped—the city buildings they were heading toward.

"For sure we can do it," Ta thought, waiting for Lekka to rise from where she had spontaneously squatted. "Particularly if there are shadows enough and if those looking don't honor their eyes."

Some Shyers back from City rotation had reported difficulty in Going Shy against concrete walls. "Something about man-made structures," they said, "or about the ratio of concrete to steel. We couldn't always get in synch with it. We usually were observed when we tried unless we could distract lookers or deepen the gloomth."

Ta wondered again what concrete and steel were if they were not motherwares? Processed, to be sure, but still of the earth. She shuddered. She was uneasy enough at having to live in the City at all, and far more uneasy at the prospect of being discovered there. And if Going Shy did not work? She shook her head to drive back the mood.

"I'd like to stay here," she thought, standing stock still on the side of a low rise. "Just slow down like the winter to a dead stop. Stay here in the whitenesses with no movement to break the air." So silent. So still. Not even the sometimes squeak of wet snow beneath their boots.

This blanket had had a new cover laid upon it almost every day. "Are they getting longer, these winters?" she asked herself, moving forward again. She eased under a branch and held it back for Lekka. "Like in the east? Sarah used to say they didn't see the ground from October to May."

Lekka's thought enfolded her musings. "Durelle says another round is blowing up. If we settle in now for the night she thinks we can start with a clearer day tomorrow, perhaps make the glade by evening."

Both women stood in the late afternoon light, Ta ranging out even as she enfolded Lekka to seek possible temporary shelter. "Another fall?" she sent. "It seems too cold."

"Trust Durelle. She's heard from the windriders at the northern heights. They say it just passed there moving too turbulently for any talking. It's a small storm but pretty active and won't disperse until it hits the lower coastal hills."

Ta nodded. "Sleep it is," she sent. "Take your hardself over that ridge and see if there's any protection on the lee side. I'll find out if any friends are awake here." She relieved Lekka of her pack, pushed a dry torpor over her own hindquarters, and sank to the ground. She leaned her shoulder on a large fir stump, aware that the other woman had passed rapidly out of sight.

The trees were profoundly hushed. She had no wish to rouse them. With tiptoe approach she eased her awareness out and down, up and around, sliding gently over entrances to tiny mounds, deeply-covered warrens, hollow holes, tightly-lodged nests, snow-hidden rock breaks. There were lots of presences, big, middle-sized and small, one or two having just eaten, others dreaming of food. All of them were sleeping or in comfortably hazy doze. She found no fear among them and worked hard to awaken none. All the patches of warm nestling bodies seemed to snuggle closer to themselves and to each other. Offering only a polite greeting, they urged her past, saying drowsily, "Sorry, no room here now." Ta envied the warmth. She smiled. "I wonder if they Spoon?" she thought.

"Oh true, oh true, but not as you do." The message enfolded her own mindstretch. Immediately wary, Ta pulled in from her open sweepspan.

"They Spoon, they Spoon, oh, how they Spoon, but not to the bellows that whistle your tune." The meanings in her head were playful, as if her communicant were teasing. Ta recognized the gambit. And its source. "They Spoon, they Spoon," the inner voice was going on, almost in a child's chant, "in June they Spoon, and moon and croon—"

Ta took a long guess and sent out an extensive ritual speech of greeting, cutting off the mindchatter and allowing no interruption. She ended with, "And now, Noble Raccoon, if you will answer me three questions we can swear a care forevermore. First, by what name may we call you? Second, where can my friend and I lie safe from tonight's storm? And third, how comes it you are so lusty in the deepest part of the winter?" She waited.

There was a short silence, then, "Gotcha! I am Roxanne, called Roxie, but only by those who contest with me at riddles and conundrums." Ta sent a shortstretched bow of acknowledgment. The voice went on. "Don't you want to know how they Spoon?"

"Another time," she sent. "Right now we need a log or at least a low tree."

"The other Spooner has found one already. She comes."

Ta drew back to her hardself and saw Lekka pushing through the hillside's embankments of snow. She opened briefly to Lekka's message. "There's a place made just for us, and just in time, in a crotch between two fallen trees. Who's with you?" Ta sent a laugh, both in the welcome of shelter and with anticipation of introducing the raccoon. She had just concocted a humorous bit of doggerel with which to initiate the fun when she sensed that the raccoon's mood had changed. Before she could adjust her meter, she and Lekka were enfolded.

"I am an amicable entity, madam, or miss, or ah, I should say good woman, who was disturbed in my afternoon's vigil by the mindrovings of your sister Spooner." Ta was about to atone for her lapse in courtesy by introducing themselves when the message continued.

"Ah, you Spooners! You need not tell me your names or your destination for I know them both. And moreover, your purpose. You are Ta and Lekka, ladies of the hills, stepping big like men and wearing your deepest voices. You are bound for the City, there to disguise yourselves as male nurses in the Breeders' Home so that you may rescue from that place both women and children who are clear-seers. Your work is dangerous and you may not succeed. For myself, I wish you well and offer whatever services I may render."

Lekka's astonishment pushed aside Ta's own. "Mother's Music!" she exclaimed aloud.

"I don't understand your shock," the raccoon went on. "Many more than I know these things. And with our knowledge we are often able to help you. You protect us, we protect you. A trade agreement. But enough. The darkness is coming and with it a quick hard snow—"

"I don't even see you," Lekka broke in.

"There. On the low limb." Ta pointed. Then to the bundle of blackness she sent, "You did not answer my last question."

"Ah yes." For a moment Ta half hoped that the animal would return to its lighter mood. But the formal tone continued. "I am awaiting some friends. I only a moment ago was disappointed to understand that they may be into the late morning coming. I shall be awake here all the night to guard their path and if you will trust me, then one of you will not have to be on light watch. You both may enjoy safe sleep. To rejoin our initial subject," added the little animal, its round eyes glowing now, "you may even sleep Spoon."

Ta closed to the animal in order to send a question to Lekka.

"Fine with me," Lekka sent back. "We're not in the valley yet and I'm a trusting soul. Why is she so hooked on Spooning?"

"I don't know." Ta again opened to the raccoon. "We are grateful for your watch," she sent.

"And," Lekka added, "we wonder how you know of our Spooning?"

The bundle of blackness shifted with impatience, perhaps even with incredulity. "I do not know whether it is your unfortunate biological classification or the inadequacies of your age," came the answer, "but something there is in you that approaches the denseness of the males of your species. It is in your Spooning that you are closest to the rest of us. That is how we know." With something of a snap of indignation the figure dismissed them, then resumed in a high soprano enfoldment, "Neither my eyes nor my ears will falter. Nor my nose nor my tail nor my throat nor my grail, nor any sense that might protect you. May the Mother grant you deep safe sleep."

"That's our exit cue," Ta sent, her eyes still taking leave of the raccoon. She picked up her pack. Lekka followed her through the fading light, up the rise and down again. Ta spread two canvas cloths over a pocket of closely packed whiteness and began gathering loose snow for their top blanket, talking as she did so to the little drifts themselves, ascertaining with each move that the element she worked with was at ease and willing.

Then Lekka sent, "Right or left, Ta?"

"Right," Ta answered.

Lekka stripped off her clothes and began making the indentations in the lower canvas for both their bodies, carefully estimating the two primary Spooning positions and settling the soft edges of their packs for the gentlest pillowings. With one mind movement she laid an extended torpor over the canvas and all their clothing, pushing dryness into every fold and corner of the area that was to be their resting place.

Ta too was naked now, shivering in the last of the light as she rolled her boots and trousers together and drove them with her feet toward the bottom of their bed. From a sitting position she began covering them both with the top canvas and heavy heaps of white warmth. Then she sent out through the darkness a last check span toward Roxanne the Regal.

"All well," came a response. Ta withdrew.

Lekka's grin was barely discernable in the shadows. "Will you Spoon with me, sister?" she said aloud.

"With pleasure, sister," said Ta also aloud.

"Right side, we decided?"

"Right side," Ta answered shifting to her right even as she pulled Lekka down to her.

The wind was up now. It had brought with it a spit of snow and a night threatening bitter cold. Ta shuddered. Lekka tucked her knees behind the larger woman's, and maneuvered her own right arm to a convenient niche between their bodies. "Arm in your way?" she sent.

"No. Just fine," Ta answered. She scrunched into the tightly molded space and pulled both canvas and snow over her shoulder to meet the packs at the tops of their heads. The new blanket seemed to know where to fall, how to resist resting on warm flesh. "Tuck my neck," she sent.

Lekka obligingly pulled a corner of whiteness between her own mouth and Ta's short black curls. At the same time with a vamp of her rump and shoulders she sucked in the covers behind her own back and rested her left arm over Ta, doubling it back a trifle so that her hand could touch Ta's left breast. Ta's hand covered Lekka's. They lay huddled now, together—shaded from the world by a cold stiffness that warmed them to the bone. Lekka pressed Ta loosely to the contours of her own angled body.

Ta sighed. They might awake, she knew, buried beneath the driftings of the coming storm. They might not awake at all. She was embarking on the darkness now, and a flow of words from another woman's life rose up to stroke her: "As freezing persons recollect the snow: first chill, then stupor, then the letting go."

"Well," she thought, "we'll go Spooning, anyway." With a smile Ta silently praised the night that she and her learntogether had discovered for themselves the magic of bare bodies, front-to-back, catapulted by the rhythm of the new-learned ritual into the deepest universe she had ever known. She and Lekka would Spoon well tonight. Already, even before they had spoken the incantatatory words, she felt the approaching seduction of the night's journey.

Then Lekka whispered aloud, "Our thanks to the cunning raccoon that we are watched and shaded."

"Our thanks to the earth and the falling snow, that we are embraced in a womb of warmth," said Ta, also in a whisper. Then she felt the rising of a chest tone as Lekka initiated and sustained a low resonant note. Her own voice matched the tone sending it back deep into her lungs. It hovered there only an instant, then moved to her abdomen, her crotch, her thighs, her legs and feet, uniting Lekka's barely moving body with her own. Breathing alternately and at long intervals the two women began to stir torsos and limbs into instruments of vibrating empathy, elongating tone after tone, in harmony, in unison, in syncopated encounter. Ta felt the darkness descend now, enclosing them both.

Lekka moved into full Spooning position, pushing Ta's buttocks into her lower belly and shifting her hand so that it met Ta's in a nest of darkness between Ta's breasts. Their mutual tones haunted each other, called after each other, echoed each other, one just behind the other until they sang together in a single simple strain:

> "I seek the darkness as of old.
> With you I trust the earth to hold
> and cradle me in worlds untold,
> to dare the death within our slumber.

> "I sink, and unencumbered spin.
> I swoop the caverns of the wind.
> I cannot tell you who my kin
> save all who do not cage another.

> "Come woman, partner of my rest,
> we join our lives in sisterquest

and plunge the hidden learningfest
where all of life has surged before us."

A low hollow whistle replaced the words. It came from every direction and widened into a plaintive moan. Each time she reached this sliding off point Ta was reminded that she never could tell where the whistling came from and that she must remember to ask Lekka if it were she who whistled.

An Old Woman
and Her Cat

DORIS LESSING

*H*er name was Hetty, and she was born with the twentieth century. She was seventy when she died of cold and malnutrition. She had been alone for a long time, since her husband had died of pneumonia in a bad winter soon after the Second World War. He had not been more than middleaged. Her four children were now middleaged, with grown children. Of these descendants one daughter sent her Christmas cards, but otherwise she did not exist for them. For they were all respectable people, with homes and good jobs and cars. And Hetty was not respectable. She had always been a bit strange, these people said, when mentioning her at all.

When Fred Pennefather, her husband, was alive and the children just growing up, they all lived much too close and uncomfortable in a Council flat in that part of London which is like an estuary, with tides of people flooding in and out: they were not half a mile from the great stations of Euston, St. Pancras, and

King's Cross. The blocks of flats were pioneers in that area, standing up grim, grey, hideous, among many acres of little houses and gardens, all soon to be demolished so that they could be replaced by more tall grey blocks. The Pennefathers were good tenants, paying their rent, keeping out of debt; he was a building worker, "steady," and proud of it. There was no evidence then of Hetty's future dislocation from the normal, unless it was that she very often slipped down for an hour or so to the platforms where the locomotives drew in and ground out again. She liked the smell of it all, she said. She liked to see people moving about, "coming and going from all those foreign places." She meant Scotland, Ireland, the North of England. These visits into the din, the smoke, the massed swirling people were for her a drug, like other people's drinking or gambling. Her husband teased her, calling her a gypsy. She was in fact part gypsy, for her mother had been one, but had chosen to leave her people and marry a man who lived in a house. Fred Pennefather liked his wife for being different from the run of the women he knew, and had married her because of it, but her children were fearful that her gypsy blood might show itself in worse ways than haunting railway stations. She was a tall woman with a lot of glossy black hair, a skin that tanned easily, and dark strong eyes. She wore bright colours, and enjoyed quick tempers and sudden reconcilia-tions. In her prime she attracted attention, was proud and hand-some. All this made it inevitable that the people in those streets should refer to her as "that gypsy woman." When she heard them, she shouted back that she was none the worse for that.

After her husband died and the children married and left, the Council moved her to a small flat in the same building. She got a job selling food in a local store, but found it boring. There seem to be traditional occupations for middleaged women living alone, the busy and responsible part of their lives being over. Drink. Gam-bling. Looking for another husband. A wistful affair or two. That's about it. Hetty went through a period of, as it were, testing out all these, like hobbies, but tired of them. While still earning her small wage as a saleswoman, she began a trade in buying and selling secondhand clothes from householders, and sold these to stalls and the secondhand shops. She adored doing this. It was a passion. She gave up her respectable job and forgot all about her love of trains and travellers. Her room was always full of bright bits of cloth, a dress that had a pattern she fancied and did not want to sell, strips of beading, old furs, embroidery, lace. There were street traders among the people in the flats, but there was something in the way Hetty went about it that lost her friends. Neighbours of twenty or thirty years' standing said she had gone queer, and wished to know her no longer. But she did not mind. She was enjoying herself too much, particularly the moving about the streets with her old perambulator, in which she crammed what she was buying or selling. She liked the gossiping, the bargaining, the wheedling from householders. It was this last which—and she knew this quite well, of course—the neighbours objected to. It was the thin edge of the wedge. It was begging. Decent people did not beg. She was no longer decent.

Lonely in her tiny flat, she was there as little as possible, always preferring the lively streets. But she had after all to spend some time in her room, and one day she saw a kitten lost and trembling in a dirty corner, and brought it home to the block of flats. She was on a fifth floor. While the kitten was growing into a large strong tom, he ranged about that conglomeration of staircases and lifts and many dozens of flats, as if the building were a town. Pets were not actively persecuted by the authorities, only forbidden and then tolerated. Hetty's life from the coming of the cat became more sociable, for the beast was always making friends with somebody in the cliff that was the block of flats across the court, or not coming home for nights at a time, so that she had to go and look for him and knock on doors and ask, or returning home kicked and limping, or bleeding after a fight with his kind. She made scenes with the kickers, or the owners of the enemy cats, exchanged cat lore with cat lovers, was always having to bandage and nurse her poor Tibby. The cat was soon a scarred warrior with fleas, a torn ear, and a ragged look to him. He was a multicoloured cat and his eyes were small and yellow.

He was a long way down the scale from the delicately coloured, elegantly shaped pedigree cats. But he was independent, and often caught himself pigeons when he could no longer stand the tinned cat food, or the bread and packet gravy Hetty fed him, and he purred and nestled when she grabbed him to her bosom at those times she suffered loneliness. This happened less and less. Once she had realised that her children were hoping that she would leave them alone because the old rag trader was an embarrassment to them, she accepted it, and a bitterness that always had wild humour in it only welled up at times like Christmas. She sang or chanted to the cat: "You nasty old beast, filthy old cat, nobody wants you, do they Tibby, no, you're just an alley tom, just an old stealing cat, hey Tibs, Tibs, Tibs."

The building teemed with cats. There were even a couple of dogs. They all fought up and down the grey cement corridors. There were sometimes dog and cat messes which someone had to clear up, but which might be left for days and weeks as part of neighbourly wars and feuds. There were many complaints. Finally an official came from the Council to say that the ruling about keeping animals was going to be enforced. Hetty, like others, would have to have her cat destroyed. This crisis coincided with a time of bad luck for her. She had had 'flu; had not been able to earn money, had found it hard to get out for her pension, had run into debt. She owed a lot of back rent, too. A television set she had hired and was not paying for attracted the visits of a television representative. The neighbours were gossiping that Hetty had "gone savage." This was because the cat had brought up the stairs and along the passageways a pigeon he had caught, shedding feathers and blood all the way; a woman coming in to complain found Hetty plucking the pigeon to stew it, as she had done with others, sharing the meal with Tibby.

"You're filthy," she would say to him, setting the stew down to cool in his dish. "Filthy old thing. Eating that dirty old pigeon. What do you think you are, a wild cat? Decent cats don't eat dirty birds. Only those old gypsies eat wild birds."

One night she begged help from a neighbour who had a car,

and put into the car herself, the television set, the cat, bundles of clothes, and the pram. She was driven across London to a room in a street that was a slum because it was waiting to be done up. The neighbour made a second trip to bring her bed and her mattress, which were tied to the roof of the car, a chest of drawers, an old trunk, saucepans. It was in this way that she left the street in which she had lived for thirty years, nearly half her life.

She set up house again in one room. She was frightened to go near "them" to re-establish pension rights and her identity, because of the arrears of rent she had left behind, and because of the stolen television set. She started trading again, and the little room was soon spread, like her last, with a rainbow of colours and textures and lace and sequins. She cooked on a single gas ring and washed in the sink. There was no hot water unless it was boiled in saucepans. There were several old ladies and a family of five children in the house, which was condemned.

She was in the ground floor back, with a window which opened onto a derelict garden, and her cat was happy in a hunting ground that was a mile around this house where his mistress was so splendidly living. A canal ran close by, and in the dirty citywater were islands which a cat could reach by leaping from moored boat to boat. On the islands were rats and birds. There were pavements full of fat London pigeons. The cat was a fine hunter. He soon had his place in the hierarchies of the local cat population and did not have to fight much to keep it. He was a strong male cat, and fathered many litters of kittens.

In that place Hetty and he lived five happy years. She was trading well, for there were rich people close by to shed what the poor needed to buy cheaply. She was not lonely, for she made a quarrelling but satisfying friendship with a woman on the top floor, a widow like herself who did not see her children either. Hetty was sharp with the five children, complaining about their noise and mess, but she slipped them bits of money and sweets after telling their mother that "she was a fool to put herself out for them, because they wouldn't appreciate it." She was living well, even without her pension. She sold the television set and gave herself and her friend upstairs some day-trips to the coast, and bought a small radio. She never read books or magazines. The truth was that she could not write or read, or only so badly it was no pleasure to her. Her cat was all reward and no cost, for he fed himself, and continued to bring in pigeons for her to cook and eat, for which in return he claimed milk.

"Greedy Tibby, you greedy *thing,* don't think I don't know, oh yes I do, you'll get sick eating those old pigeons, I do keep telling you that, don't I"

At last the street was being done up. No longer a uniform, long, disgraceful slum, houses were being bought by the middle-class people. While this meant more good warm clothes for trad-ing—or begging, for she still could not resist the attraction of get-ting something for nothing by the use of her plaintive inventive tongue, her still-flashing handsome eyes—Hetty knew, like her neighbours, that soon this house with its cargo of poor people would be bought for improvement.

In the week Hetty was seventy years old came the notice that was the end of this little community. They had four weeks to find somewhere else to live.

Usually, the shortage of housing being what it is in London—and everywhere else in the world, of course—these people would have had to scatter, fending for themselves. But the fate of this particular street was attracting attention, because a municipal election was pending. Homelessness among the poor was finding a focus in this street which was a perfect symbol of the whole area, and indeed the whole city, half of it being fine converted tasteful houses, full of people who spent a lot of money, and half being dying houses tenanted by people like Hetty.

As a result of speeches by councillors and churchmen, local authorities found themselves unable to ignore the victims of this redevelopment. The people in the house Hetty was in were visited by a team consisting of an unemployment officer, a social worker, and a rehousing officer. Hetty, a strong gaunt old woman wearing a scarlet wool suit she had found among her cast-offs that week, a black knitted teacosy on her head, and black buttoned Edwardian boots too big for her, so that she had to shuffle, invited them into her room. But although all were well used to the extremes of poverty, none wished to enter the place, but stood in the doorway and made her this offer: that she should be aided to get her pension—why had she not claimed it long ago?—and that she, together with the four other old ladies in the house, should move to a Home run by the Council out in the northern suburbs. All these women were used to, and enjoyed, lively London, and while they had no alternative but to agree, they fell into a saddened and sullen state. Hetty agreed too. The last two winters had set her bones aching badly, and a cough was never far away. And while perhaps she was more an urban soul even than the others, since she had walked up and down so many streets with her old perambulator loaded with rags and laces, and since she knew so intimately London's texture and taste, she minded least of all the idea of a new home "among green fields." There were, in fact, no fields near the promised Home, but for some reason all the old ladies had chosen to bring out this old song of a phrase, as if it belonged to their situation, that of old women not far off death. "It will be nice to be near green fields again," they said to each other over cups of tea.

The housing officer came to make final arrangements. Hetty Pennefather was to move with the others in two weeks' time. The young man, sitting on the very edge of the only chair in the crammed room, because it was greasy and he suspected it had fleas or worse in it, breathed as lightly as he could because of the appalling stink: there was a lavatory in the house, but it had been out of order for three days, and it was just the other side of a thin wall. The whole house smelled.

The young man, who knew only too well the extent of the misery due to lack of housing, who knew how many old people abandoned by their children did not get the offer to spend their days being looked after by the authorities, could not help feeling that this wreck of a human being could count herself lucky to get a place in this "Home," even if it was—and he knew and deplored the fact—an institution in which the old were treated like naughty and dimwitted children until they had the good fortune to die.

But just as he was telling Hetty that a van would be coming to take her effects and those of the other four old ladies, and that she need not take anything more with her than her clothes "and perhaps a few photographs," he saw what he had thought was a heap of multicoloured rags get up and put its ragged gingeryblack paws on the old woman's skirt. Which today was a cretonne curtain covered with pink and red roses that Hetty had pinned around her because she liked the pattern.

"You can't take that cat with you," he said automatically. It was something he had to say often, and knowing what misery the statement caused, he usually softened it down. But he had been taken by surprise.

Tibby now looked like a mass of old wool that has been matting together in dust and rain. One eye was permanently half-closed, because a muscle had been ripped in a fight. One ear was vestigial. And down a flank was a hairless slope with a thick scar on it. A cat-hating man had treated Tibby as he treated all cats, to a pellet from his airgun. The resulting wound had taken two years to heal. And Tibby smelled.

No worse, however, than his mistress, who sat stiffly still, bright-eyed with suspicion, hostile, watching the well-brushed tidy young man from the Council.

"How old is that beast?"

"Ten years, no, only eight years, he's a young cat about five years old," said Hetty, desperate.

"It looks as if you'd do him a favour to put him out of his misery," said the young man.

When the official left, Hetty had agreed to everything. She was the only one of the old women with a cat. The others had budgerigars or nothing. Budgies were allowed in the Home.

She made her plans, confided in the others, and when the van came for them and their clothes and photographs and budgies, she was not there, and they told lies for her. "Oh we don't know where she can have gone, dear," the old women repeated again and again to the indifferent van driver. "She was here last night, but she did say something about going to her daughter in Manchester." And off they went to die in the Home.

Hetty knew that when houses have been emptied for redevelopment they may stay empty for months, even years. She intended to go on living in this one until the builders moved in.

It was a warm autumn. For the first time in her life she lived like her gypsy forebears, and did not go to bed in a room in a house like respectable people. She spent several nights, with Tibby, sitting crouched in a doorway of an empty house two doors from her own. She knew exactly when the police would come around, and where to hide herself in the bushes of the overgrown shrubby garden.

As she had expected, nothing happened in the house, and she moved back in. She smashed a back windowpane so that Tibby could move in and out without her having to unlock the front door for him, and without leaving a window suspiciously open. She moved to the top back room and left it every morning early, to spend the day in the streets with her pram and her rags. At night she kept a candle glimmering low down on the floor. The lavatory was still out of order, so she used a pail on the first floor, instead, and secretly emptied it at night into the canal, which in the day was full of pleasure boats and people fishing.

Tibby brought her several pigeons during that time.

"Oh you are a clever puss, Tibby, Tibby! Oh you're clever, you are. You know how things are, don't you, you know how to get around and about."

The weather turned very cold; Christmas came and went. Hetty's cough came back, and she spent most of her time under piles of blankets and old clothes, dozing. At night she watched the shadows of the candle flame on floor and ceiling—the windowframes fitted badly, and there was a draught. Twice tramps spent the night in the bottom of the house and she heard them being moved on by the police. She had to go down to make sure the police had not blocked up the broken window the cat used, but they had not. A black bird had flown in and had battered itself to death trying to get out. She plucked it, and roasted it over a fire made with bits of floorboard in a baking pan: the gas of course had been cut off. She had never eaten very much, and was not frightened that some dry bread and a bit of cheese was all that she had eaten during her sojourn under the heap of clothes. She was cold, but did not think about that much. Outside there was slushy brown snow everywhere. She went back to her nest thinking that soon the cold spell would be over and she could get back to her trading. Tibby sometimes got into the pile with her, and she clutched the warmth of him to her. "Oh you clever cat, you clever old thing, looking after yourself, aren't you? That's right my ducky, that's right my lovely."

And then, just as she was moving about again, with snow gone off the ground for a time but winter only just begun, in January, she saw a builder's van draw up outside, a couple of men unloading their gear. They did not come into the house: they were to start work next day. By then Hetty, her cat, her pram piled with clothes and her two blankets, were gone. She also took a box of matches, a candle, an old saucepan and a fork and spoon, a tinopener, and a rat-trap. She had a horror of rats.

About two miles away, among the homes and gardens of amiable Hampstead, where live so many of the rich, the intelligent and the famous, stood three empty, very large houses. She had seen them on an occasion, a couple of years before, when she had taken a bus. This was a rare thing for her, because of the remarks and curious looks provoked by her mad clothes, and by her being able to appear at the same time such a tough battling old thing and a naughty child. For the older she got, this disreputable tramp, the more there strengthened in her a quality of fierce, demanding childishness. It was all too much of a mixture; she was uncomfortable to have near.

She was afraid that "they" might have rebuilt the houses, but there they still stood, too tumbledown and dangerous to be of much use to tramps, let alone the armies of London's homeless. There was no glass left anywhere. The flooring at ground level was mostly gone, leaving small platforms and juts of planking

over basements full of water. The ceilings were crumbling. The
roofs were going. The houses were like bombed buildings.

But on the cold dark of a late afternoon she pulled the pram
up the broken stairs and moved cautiously around the frail boards
of a second-floor room that had a great hole in it right down to
the bottom of the house. Looking into it was like looking into a
well. She held a candle to examine the state of the walls, here
more or less whole, and saw that rain and wind blowing in from
the window would leave one corner dry. Here she made her
home. A sycamore tree screened the gaping window from the
main road twenty yards away. Tibby, who was cramped after
making the journey under the clothes piled in the pram, bounded
down and out and vanished into neglected undergrowth to catch
his supper. He returned fed and pleased, and seemed happy to
stay clutched in her hard thin old arms. She had come to watch
for his return after hunting trips, because the warm purring
bundle of bones and fur did seem to allay, for a while, the permanent ache of cold in her bones.

Next day she sold her Edwardian boots for a few shillings —
they were fashionable again — and bought a loaf and some bacon
scraps. In a corner of the ruins well away from the one she had
made her own, she pulled up some floorboards, built a fire, and
toasted bread and the bacon scraps. Tibby had brought in a
pigeon, and she roasted that, but not very efficiently. She was
afraid of the fire catching and the whole mass going up in flames;
she was afraid of too much of the smoke showing and attracting
the police. She had to keep damping down the fire, and so the
bird was bloody and unappetising, and in the end Tibby got most
of it. She felt confused, and discouraged, but thought it was
because of the long stretch of winter still ahead of her before
spring could come. In fact, she was ill. She made a couple of attempts to trade and earn money to feed herself before she
acknowledged she was ill. She knew she was not yet dangerously
ill, for she had been that in her life, and would have been able to
recognise the cold listless indifference of a real last-ditch illness.
But all her bones ached, and her head ached, and she coughed

more than she ever had. Yet she still did not think of herself as suffering particularly from the cold, even in that sleety January weather. She had never, in all her life, lived in a properly heated place, had never known a really warm home, not even when she lived in the Council flats. Those flats had electric fires, and the family had never used them, for the sake of economy, except in very bad spells of cold. They piled clothes onto themselves, or went to bed early. But she did know that to keep herself from dying now she could not treat the cold with her usual indifference. She knew she must eat. In the comparatively dry corner of the windy room, away from the gaping window through which snow and sleet were drifting, she made another nest—her last. She had found a piece of plastic sheeting in the rubble, and she laid that down first, so that the damp would not strike up. Then she spread her two blankets over that. Over them were heaped the mass of old clothes. She wished she had another piece of plastic to put on top, but she used sheets of newspaper instead. She heaved herself into the middle of this, with a loaf of bread near to her hand. She dozed, and waited, and nibbled bits of bread, and watched the snow drifting softly in. Tibby sat close to the old blue face that poked out of the pile and put up a paw to touch it. He miaowed and was restless, and then went out into the frosty morning and brought in a pigeon. This the cat put, still struggling and fluttering a little, close to the old woman. But she was afraid to get out of the pile in which the heat was being made and kept with such difficulty. She really could not climb out long enough to pull up more splinters of plank from the floors, to make a fire, to pluck the pigeon, to roast it. She put out a cold hand to stroke the cat.

"Tibby, you old thing, you brought it for me then, did you? You did, did you? Come here, come in here. . . ." But he did not want to get in with her. He miaowed again, pushed the bird closer to her. It was now limp and dead.

"You have it then. You eat it. I'm not hungry, thank you Tibby."

But the carcase did not interest him. He had eaten a pigeon

before bringing this one up to Hetty. He fed himself well. In spite of his matted fur, and his scars and his half-closed yellow eye, he was a strong healthy cat.

At about four the next morning there were steps and voices downstairs. Hetty shot out of the pile and crouched behind a fallen heap of plaster and beams, now covered with snow, at the end of the room near the window. She could see through the hole in the floorboards down to the first floor, which had collapsed entirely, and through it to the ground floor. She saw a man in a thick overcoat and muffler and leather gloves holding a strong torch to illuminate a thin bundle of clothes lying on the floor. She saw that this bundle was a sleeping man or woman. She was indignant—her home was being trespassed upon. And she was afraid because she had not been aware of this other tenant of the ruin. Had he, or she, heard her talking to the cat? And where was the cat? If he wasn't careful he would be caught, and that would be the end of him. The man with a torch went off and came back with a second man. In the thick dark far below Hetty saw a small cave of strong light, which was the torchlight. In this space of light two men bent to lift the bundle, carried it out across the dangertraps of fallen and rotting boards that made gangplanks over the water-filled basements. One man was holding the torch in the hand that supported the dead person's feet, and the light jogged and lurched over trees and grasses: the corpse was being taken through the shrubberies to a car.

There are men in London who, between the hours of two and five in the morning—when the real citizens are asleep, who should not be disturbed by such unpleasantness as the corpses of the poor—make the rounds of all the empty, rotting houses they know about, to collect the dead, and to warn the living that they ought not to be there at all, inviting them to one of the official Homes or lodgings for the homeless.

Hetty was too frightened to get back into her warm heap. She sat with the blankets pulled around her, and looked through gaps in the fabric of the house, making out shapes and boundaries and holes and puddles and mounds of rubble, as her eyes, like her cat's, became accustomed to the dark.

She heard scuffling sounds and knew they were rats. She had meant to set the trap, but the thought of her friend Tibby, who might catch his paw, had stopped her. She sat up until the morning light came in grey and cold, after nine. Now she did know herself to be very ill and in danger, for she had lost all the warmth she had huddled into her bones under the rags. She shivered violently. She was shaking herself apart with shivering. In between spasms she drooped limp and exhausted. Through the ceiling above her—but it was not a ceiling, only a cobweb of slats and planks—she could see into a dark cave which had been a garret, and through the roof above that, the grey sky, teeming with incipient rain. The cat came back from where he had been hiding, and sat crouched on her knees, keeping her stomach warm, while she thought out her position. These were her last clear thoughts. She told herself that she would not last out until spring unless she allowed "them" to find her, and take her to hospital. After that, she would be taken to a Home.

But what would happen to Tibby, her poor cat? She rubbed the old beast's scruffy head with the ball of her thumb and muttered: "Tibby, Tibby, they won't get you, no, you'll be all right, yes, I'll look after you."

Towards midday, the sun oozed yellow through miles of greasy grey cloud, and she staggered down the rotting stairs, to the shops. Even in those London streets, where the extraordinary has become usual, people turned to stare at a tall gaunt woman, with a white face that had flaming red patches on it, and blue compressed lips, and restless black eyes. She wore a tightly buttoned man's overcoat, torn brown woollen mittens, and an old fur hood. She pushed a pram loaded with old dresses and scraps of embroidery and torn jerseys and shoes, all stirred into a tight tangle, and she kept pushing this pram up against people as they stood in queues, or gossiped, or stared into windows, and she muttered: "Give me your old clothes darling, give me your old pretties, give Hetty something, poor Hetty's hungry." A woman gave her a handful of small change, and Hetty bought a roll filled with tomato and lettuce. She did not dare go into a cafe, for even in her confused state she knew she would offend, and would probably be asked to leave. But she begged a cup of tea at a street stall, and when the hot sweet liquid flooded through her she felt she might survive the winter. She bought a carton of milk and pushed the pram back through the slushy snowy street to the ruins.

Tibby was not there. She urinated down through the gap in the boards, muttering, "A nuisance, that old tea," and wrapped herself in a blanket and waited for the dark to come.

Tibby came in later. He had blood on his foreleg. She had heard scuffling and she knew that he had fought a rat, or several, and had been bitten. She poured the milk into the tilted saucepan and Tibby drank it all.

She spent the night with the animal held against her chilly bosom. They did not sleep, but dozed off and on. Tibby would normally be hunting, the night was his time, but he had stayed with the old woman now for three nights.

Early next morning they again heard the corpse removers among the rubble on the ground floor, and saw the beams of the torch moving on wet walls and collapsed beams. For a moment the torchlight was almost straight on Hetty, but no one came up: who could believe that a person could be desperate enough to climb those dangerous stairs, to trust those crumbling splintery floors, and in the middle of winter?

Hetty had now stopped thinking of herself as ill, of the degrees of her illness, of her danger—of the impossibility of her surviving. She had cancelled out in her mind the presence of winter and its lethal weather, and it was as if spring were nearly here. She knew that if it had been spring when she had had to leave the other house, she and the cat could have lived here for months and months, quite safely and comfortably. Because it seemed to her an impossible and even a silly thing that her life, or, rather, her death, could depend on something so arbitrary as builders starting work on a house in January rather than in April, she could not believe it: the fact would not stay in her mind. The day before she had been quite clearheaded. But today her thoughts were cloudy, and she talked and laughed aloud. Once she scrambled up and rummaged in her rags for an old Christmas card she had got four years before from her good daughter.

In a hard harsh angry grumbling voice she said to her four children that she needed a room of her own now that she was getting on. "I've been a good mother to you," she shouted to them before invisible witnesses—former neighbours, welfare workers, a doctor. "I never let you want for anything, never! When you were little you always had the best of everything! You can ask anybody; go on, ask them, then!"

She was restless and made such a noise that Tibby left her and bounded on to the pram and crouched watching her. He was limping, and his foreleg was rusty with blood. The rat had bitten deep. When the daylight came, he left Hetty in a kind of sleep, and went down into the garden where he saw a pigeon feeding on the edge of the pavement. The cat pounced on the bird, dragged it into the bushes, and ate it all, without taking it up to his mistress. After he had finished eating, he stayed hidden, watching the passing people. He stared at them intently with his blazing yellow eye, as if he were thinking, or planning. He did not go into the old ruin and up the crumbling wet stairs until late—it was as if he knew it was not worth going at all.

He found Hetty, apparently asleep, wrapped loosely in a blanket, propped sitting in a corner. Her head had fallen on her chest, and her quantities of white hair had escaped from a scarlet woollen cap, and concealed a face that was flushed a deceptive pink—the flush of coma from cold. She was not yet dead, but she died that night. The rats came up the walls and along the planks and the cat fled down and away from them, limping still, into the bushes.

Hetty was not found for a couple of weeks. The weather changed to warm, and the man whose job it was to look for corpses was led up the dangerous stairs by the smell. There was something left of her, but not much.

As for the cat, he lingered for two or three days in the thick shrubberies, watching the passing people and beyond them, the thundering traffic of the main road. Once a couple stopped to talk on the pavement, and the cat, seeing two pairs of legs, moved out and rubbed himself against one of the legs. A hand came down and he was stroked and patted for a little. Then the people went away.

The cat saw he would not find another home, and he moved off, nosing and feeling his way from one garden to another, through empty houses, finally into an old churchyard. This graveyard already had a couple of stray cats in it, and he joined them. It was the beginning of a community of stray cats going wild. They killed birds, and the field mice that lived among the grasses, and they drank from puddles. Before winter had ended the cats had had a hard time of it from thirst, during the two long spells when the ground froze and there was snow and no puddles and the birds were hard to catch because the cats were so easy to see against the clean white. But on the whole they managed quite well. One of the cats was female, and soon there were a swarm of wild cats, as wild as if they did not live in the middle of a city surrounded by streets and houses. This was just one of half a dozen communities of wild cats living in that square mile of London.

Then an official came to trap the cats and take them away. Some of them escaped, hiding till it was safe to come back again. But Tibby was caught. He was not only getting old and stiff—he still limped from the rat's bite—but he was friendly, and did not run away from the man, who had only to pick him up in his arms.

"You're an old soldier, aren't you?" said the man. "A real tough one, a real old tramp."

It is possible that the cat even thought that he might be finding another human friend and a home.

But it was not so. The haul of wild cats that week numbered hundreds, and while if Tibby had been younger a home might have been found for him, since he was amiable, and wished to be liked by the human race, he was really too old, and smelly and battered. So they gave him an injection and, as we say, "put him to sleep."

The Muskrat

ANNIE DILLARD

*L*earning to stalk muskrats took me several years.

I've always known there were muskrats in the creek. Sometimes when I drove late at night my headlights' beam on the water would catch the broad lines of ripples made by a swimming muskrat, a bow wave, converging across the water at the raised dark vee of its head. I would stop the car and get out: nothing. They eat corn and tomatoes from my neighbors' gardens, too, by night, so that my neighbors were always telling me that the creek was full of them. Around here, people call them "mushrats"; Thoreau called them "Musquashes." They are not of course rats at all (let alone squashes). They are more like diminutive beavers, and, like beavers, they exude a scented oil from musk glands under the base of the tail—hence the name. I had read in several respectable sources that muskrats are so wary they are almost im-

---

Excerpted from *Pilgrim at Tinker Creek* (Harper & Row, Publishers).

possible to observe. One expert who made a full-time study of large populations, mainly by examining "sign" and performing autopsies on corpses, said he often went for weeks at a time without seeing a single living muskrat.

One hot evening three years ago, I was standing more or less *in* a bush. I was stock-still, looking deep into Tinker Creek from a spot on the bank oposite the house, watching a group of bluegills stare and hang motionless near the bottom of a deep, sunlit pool. I was focused for depth. I had long since lost myself, lost the creek, the day, lost everything but still amber depth. All at once I couldn't see. And then I could: a young muskrat had appeared on top of the water, floating on its back. Its forelegs were folded langorously across its chest; the sun shone on its upturned belly. Its youthfulness and rodent grin, coupled with its ridiculous method of locomotion, which consisted of a lazy wag of the tail assisted by an occasional dabble of a webbed hind foot, made it an enchanting picture of decadence, dissipation, and summer sloth. I forgot all about the fish.

But in my surprise at having the light come on so suddenly, and at having my consciousness returned to me all at once and bearing an inverted muskrat, I must have moved and betrayed myself. The kit—for I know now it was just a young kit—righted itself so that only its head was visible above water, and swam downstream, away from me. I extricated myself from the bush and foolishly pursued it. It dove sleekly, reemerged, and glided for the opposite bank. I ran along the bankside brush, trying to keep it in sight. It kept casting an alarmed look over its shoulder at me. Once again it dove, under a floating mat of brush lodged in the bank, and disappeared. I never saw it again. (Nor have I ever, despite all the muskrats I have seen, again seen a muskrat floating on its back.) But I did not know muskrats then; I waited panting, and watched the shadowed bank. Now I know that I cannot out-wait a muskrat who knows I am there. The most I can do is get "there" quietly, while it is still in its hole, so that it never knows, and wait there until it emerges. But then all I knew was that I wanted to see more muskrats.

I began to look for them day and night. Sometimes I would see ripples suddenly start beating from the creek's side, but as I crouched to watch, the ripples would die. Now I know what this means, and have learned to stand perfectly still to make out the muskrat's small, pointed face hidden under overhanging bank vegetation, watching me. That summer I haunted the bridges, I walked up creeks and down, but no muskrats ever appeared. You must just have to be there, I thought. You must have to spend the rest of your life standing in bushes. It was a once-in-a-lifetime thing, and you've had your once.

Then one night I saw another, and my life changed. After that I knew where they were in numbers, and I knew when to look. It was late dusk; I was driving home from a visit with friends. Just on the off chance I parked quietly by the creek, walked out on the narrow bridge over the shallows, and looked upstream. Someday, I had been telling myself for weeks, someday a muskrat is going to swim right through that channel in the cattails, and I am going to see it. That is precisely what happened. I looked up into the channel for a muskrat, and there it came, swimming right toward me. Knock; seek; ask. It seemed to swim with a side-to-side, sculling motion of its vertically flattened tail. It looked bigger than the upside-down muskrat, and its face more reddish. In its mouth it clasped a twig of tulip tree. One thing amazed me: it swam right down the middle of the creek. I thought it would hide in the brush along the edge; instead, it plied the waters as obviously as an aquaplane. I could just look and look.

But I was standing on the bridge, not sitting, and it saw me. It changed its course, veered towards the bank, and disappeared behind an indentation in the rushy shoreline. I felt a rush of such pure energy I thought I would not need to breathe for days.

That innocence of mine is mostly gone now, although I felt almost the same pure rush last night. I have seen many muskrats since I learned to look for them in that part of the creek. But still I seek them out in the cool of the evening, and still I hold my breath when rising ripples surge from under the creek's bank. The great hurrah about wild animals is that they exist at all, and the greater hurrah is the actual moment of seeing them. Because they have a nice dignity, and prefer to have nothing to do with me, not even as the simple objects of my vision. They show me by their very wariness what a prize it is simply to open my eyes and behold.

Muskrats are the bread and butter of the carnivorous food chain. They are like rabbits and mice: if you are big enough to eat mammals, you eat them. Hawks and owls prey on them, and foxes; so do otters. Minks are their special enemies; minks live near large muskrat populations, slinking in and out of their dens and generally hanging around like mantises outside a beehive. Muskrats are also subject to a contagious blood disease that wipes out whole colonies. Sometimes, however, their whole populations explode, just like lemmings', which are their near kin; and they either die by the hundreds or fan out across the land migrating to new creeks and ponds.

Men kill them, too. One Eskimo who hunted muskrats for a few weeks each year strictly as a sideline says that in fourteen years he killed 30,739 muskrats. The pelts sell, and the price is rising. Muskrats are the most important fur animal on the North American continent. I don't know what they bring on the Mackenzie River delta these days, but around here, fur dealers, who paid $2.90 in 1971, now pay $5.00 a pelt. They make the pelts into coats, calling the fur anything but muskrat: "Hudson seal" is typical. In the old days, after they had sold the skins, trappers would sell the meat, too, calling it "marsh rabbit." Many people still stew muskrat.

Keeping ahead of all this slaughter, a female might have as many as five litters a year, and each litter contains six or seven or more muskrats. The nest is high and dry under the bank; only the entrance is under water, usually by several feet, to foil enemies. Here the nests are marked by simple holes in a creek's clay bank; in other parts of the country muskrats build floating, conical winter lodges which are not only watertight, but edible to muskrats.

The very young have a risky life. For one thing, even snakes and raccoons eat them. For another, their mother is easily confused, and may abandon one or two of a big litter here or there, forgetting as it were to count noses. The newborn hanging on their mother's teats may drop off if the mother has to make a sudden dive into the water, and sometimes these drown. The just-weaned young have a rough time, too, because new litters are coming along so hard and fast that they have to be weaned before they really know how to survive. And if the just-weaned young are near starving, they might eat the newborn—if they can get to them. Adult muskrats, including their own mothers, often kill them if they approach too closely. But if they live through all these hazards, they can begin a life of swimming at twilight and munching cattail roots, clover, and an occasional crayfish. Paul Errington, a usually solemn authority, writes, "The muskrat nearing the end of its first month may be thought of as an independent enterprise in a very modest way."

The wonderful thing about muskrats in my book is that they cannot see very well, and are rather dim, to boot. They are extremely wary if they know I am there, and will outwait me every time. But with a modicum of skill and a minimum loss of human dignity, such as it is, I can be right "there," and the breathing fact of my presence will never penetrate their narrow skulls.

What happened last night was not only the ultimate in muskrat dimness, it was also the ultimate in human intrusion, the limit beyond which I am certain I cannot go. I would never have imagined I could go that far, actually to sit beside a feeding muskrat as beside a dinner partner at a crowded table.

What happened was this. Just in the past week I have been frequenting a different place, one of the creek's nameless feeder streams. It is mostly a shallow trickle joining several pools up to three feet deep. Over one of these pools is a tiny pedestrian bridge known locally, if at all, as the troll bridge. I was sitting on the troll bridge about an hour before sunset, looking upstream about eight feet to my right where I know the muskrats have a den. I had just lighted a cigarette when a pulse of ripples appeared at the mouth of the den, and a muskrat emerged. He swam straight toward me and headed under the bridge.

Now the moment a muskrat's eyes disappear from view under a bridge, I go into action. I have about five seconds to switch myself around so that I will be able to see him very well when he emerges on the other side of the bridge. I can easily hang my head over the other side of the bridge, so that when he appears from under me, I will be able to count his eyelashes if I want. The trouble with this maneuver is that, once his beady eyes appear again on the other side, I am stuck. If I move again, the show is over for the evening. I have to remain in whatever insane position I happen to be caught, for as long as I am in his sight, so that I stiffen all my muscles, bruise my ankles on the concrete, and burn my fingers on the cigarette. And if the muskrat goes out on a bank to feed, there I am with my face hanging a foot over the water, unable to see anything but crayfish. So I have learned to take it easy on these five-second flings.

When the muskrat went under the bridge, I moved so I could face downstream comfortably. He reappeared, and I had a good look at him. He was eight inches long in the body, and another six in the tail. Muskrat tails are black and scaled, flattened not horizontally, like beavers' tails, but vertically, like a belt stood on edge. In the winter, muskrats' tails sometimes freeze solid, and the animals chew off the frozen parts up to about an inch of the body. They must swim entirely with their hind feet, and have a terrible time steering. This one used his tail as a rudder and only occasionally as a propeller; mostly he swam with a pedaling motion of his hind feet, held very straight and moving down and around, "toeing down" like a bicycle racer. The soles of his hind feet were strangely pale; his toenails were pointed in long cones. He kept his forelegs still, tucked up to his chest.

The muskrat clambered out on the bank across the stream from me, and began feeding. He chomped down on a ten-inch weed, pushing it into his mouth steadily with both forepaws as a carpenter feeds a saw. I could hear his chewing; it sounded like somebody eating celery sticks. Then he slid back into the water with the weed still in his mouth, crossed under the bridge, and, instead of returning to his den, rose erect on a submerged rock and calmly polished off the rest of the weed. He was about four feet away from me. Immediately he swam under the bridge again, hauled himself out on the bank, and unerringly found the same spot on the grass, where he devoured the weed's stump.

All this time I was not only doing an elaborate about-face every time his eyes disappeared under the bridge, but I was also smoking a cigarette. He never noticed that the configuration of the bridge metamorphosed utterly every time he went under it. Many animals are the same way: they can't see a thing unless it's moving. Similarly, every time he turned his head away, I was free to smoke the cigarette, although of course I never knew when he would suddenly turn again and leave me caught in some wretched position. The galling thing was, he was downwind of me and my cigarette: was I really going through all this for a creature without any sense whatsoever?

After the weed stump was gone, the muskrat began ranging over the grass with a nervous motion, chewing off mouthfuls of grass and clover near the base. Soon he had gathered a huge, bushy mouthful; he pushed into the water, crossed under the bridge, swam towards his den, and dove.

When he launched himself again shortly, having apparently cached the grass, he repeated the same routine in a businesslike fashion, and returned with another shock of grass.

Out he came again. I lost him for a minute when he went under the bridge; he did not come out where I expected him. Suddenly to my utter disbelief he appeared on the bank next to me. The troll bridge itself is on a level with the low bank; there I was, and there he was, at my side. I could have touched him with the palm of my hand without straightening my elbow. He was ready to hand.

Foraging beside me he walked very humped up, maybe to

save heat loss through evaporation. Generally, whenever he was out of water he assumed the shape of a shmoo; his shoulders were as slender as a kitten's. He used his forepaws to part clumps of grass extremely tidily; I could see the flex in his narrow wrists. He gathered mouthfuls of grass and clover less by actually gnaw-ing than by biting hard near the ground, locking his neck muscles, and pushing up jerkily with his forelegs.

His jaw was underslung, his black eyes close set and glisten-ing, his small ears pointed and furred. I will have to try and see if he can cock them. I could see the water-slicked long hairs of his coat, which gathered in rich brown strands that emphasized the smooth contours of his body, and which parted to reveal the paler, softer hair like rabbit fur underneath. Despite his closeness, I never saw his teeth or belly.

After several minutes of rummaging about in the grass at my side, he eased into the water under the bridge and paddled to his den with the jawful of grass held high, and that was the last I saw of him.

In the forty minutes I watched him, he never saw me, smelled me, or heard me at all. When he was in full view of course I never moved except to breathe. My eyes would move, too, following his, but he never noticed. I even swallowed a couple of times: nothing. The swallowing thing interested me because I had read that, when you are trying to hand-tame wild birds, if you in-advertently swallow, you ruin everything. The bird, according to this theory, thinks you are swallowing in anticipation, and off it goes. The muskrat never twitched. Only once, when he was feeding from the opposite bank about eight feet away from me, did he suddenly rise upright, all alert—and then he immediately resumed foraging. But he never knew I was there.

I never knew I was there, either. For that forty minutes last night I was as purely sensitive and mute as a photographic plate; I received impressions, but I did not print out captions. My own self-awareness had disappeared; it seems now almost as though, had I been wired with electrodes, my EEG would have been flat. I have done this sort of thing so often that I have lost self-consciousness about moving slowly and halting suddenly; it is second nature to me now. And I have often noticed that even a few minutes of this self-forgetfulness is tremendously in-vigorating. I wonder if we do not waste most of our energy just by spending every waking minute saying hello to ourselves. Mar-tin Buber quotes an old Hasid master who said, "When you walk across the fields with your mind pure and holy, then from all the stones, and all growing things, and all animals, the sparks of their soul come out and cling to you, and then they are purified and become a holy fire in you." This is one way of describing the energy that comes, using the specialized Kabbalistic vocabulary of Hasidism.

I have tried to show muskrats to other people, but it rarely works. No matter how quiet we are, the muskrats stay hidden. Maybe they sense the tense hum of consciousness, the buzz from two human beings who in the silence cannot help but be aware of each other, and so of themselves. Then too, the other people in-variably suffer from a self-consciousness that prevents their stalk-ing well. It used to bother me, too: I just could not bear to lose so much dignity that I would completely alter my whole way of be-ing for a muskrat. So I would move or look around or scratch my nose, and no muskrats would show, leaving me alone with my dignity for days on end, until I decided that it was worth my while to learn—from the muskrats themselves—how to stalk.

Telepathic Rein

LOU ROBINSON

When Annie was nine, her father's mother said, "Promise you'll never smoke or marry a black man and we'll buy you a pony." That was the only time she ever smoked, fourth grade. Rode the new red pony back to the woods and lit up a Kent. She rode on a Souix Indian saddle or bareback all over Delaware County, Ohio—down to the Scioto River, on the cinder path along the tracks racing trains, through the pine woods and forgotten cemetery (where she and the mare once saw a shock-white mule standing stock still by a tombstone). She never married a black man. Never married a white man, either.

Annie had a boyfriend once who said, "Why does everything you write have to have a horse in it?" It wasn't true then, but she has made it true ever since. Why not? Keep in sight their suffering, their rebellions, their secret languages. They were both under siege, Annie and the horses. They were at the mercy. Terrible things happen to animals in the country. They pay for people's crimes.

Once she saw a TV show about a woman psychic who could read the minds of hurt racehorses. They tell her what is wrong with them. They send pictures into her head: of the brush jump that tore the tendon. . . . Do they show her the tiny wire tightened under the pastern, and who put it there? It could be a dangerous job. It would be to see a trail of tears. The original trail of tears.

When the Nez Pearce were driven back across the Snake River to the reservation, they hitched their horses to rafts. No people were lost, but thousands of Appaloosas drowned in the crossing. Annie is full of this kind of lore. She speaks with authority. "Under the auspices of" used to mean under the apron that held the oracular snake. The snake speaks with the voices of the drowned, everywhere. A person who can talk to horses can talk to snakes and is called a whisperer. Their fate is spelled in every horse's eye if you know how to read it, Annie will tell you.

They still have whisperers in Wales. A couple in Carmarthenshire have what they call a telepathic rein on their ponies. They have experimented for twenty years and can say without a doubt that there is telepathy between horses and people, and of course between horse and horse. They say their ponies' sign language is easy to understand, but the sounds take longer. Their daughter took Annie out to show her the white pony. "I have a horse at home in Ohio," Annie said. Her traveling companions, her two closest friends, stared at her, dumbstruck. She hadn't lived in Ohio for seven years, and the horse had been gone for eight. The white sight had wiped out the intervening days. It's a special kind of female fit. Everybody always said Annie had the tendency and the flair.

No one will dispute that girls and women are connected to horses since the beginning when someone drew horses coming out of her skirt on the cave walls. Or that blood is a part of it, and sex. Men may worry, including the Pope, who in the 1400s tried to outlaw women worshipping in the cave with the horse paintings. Ancient kings of Sweden were torn to pieces by horse-masked priestesses. The horseshoe over the door in Ireland, Scotland, and Wales is the Great Gate of death and rebirth, a vulva.

Annie first discovered pleasure with her pony, though she didn't have the word vulva, or any word, to describe the place between her legs where it started. Sprawled face-down across his spine one summer afternoon, head buried in his cottony mane, legs dangling down either side of his sun-warmed body that rocked in short little tugs as he grazed, she felt a warm ticklish ache in her groin grow full, fuller. Then the ache rose swift and boneless as a snake from between her legs up through her whole body to her face. A moment of intense disorientation followed, during which she groped for her name, the day of the week. She thought of it as an accident—a combination of warm sun and carelessness. The same as when you laugh so hard you wet your pants. She recreated it several times when all the elements were at hand—late afternoon sun, the pony in a lazy, grazing mood. She thought he liked it, too. Unlike laughing too hard, she believed this current originated in the pony. Much later, when she learned to use her fingers, the memory remained a potent aphrodisiac. She had only to think of her legs and arms dangling spread-eagled down the indifferent animal's back, the gentle tug and sway.

She never connected it with horse sex, which to Annie was the most brutal thing ever engineered by man (the only kind she'd ever seen). They put a twitch (a short chain on the end of a club) around the soft part of the mare's upper lip, the only place that hurts enough to hold her still, while the stallion, which she is not allowed to see, rams her from behind. The stallion has been pent up in a stall for days until he is a crazed creature that doesn't remember who you are. Both scream as if they are being slaughtered. Then they separate them. She believed that with her hands and body she could offer a better substitute. It wasn't the phallic aspect of the horse Annie worshipped, though she couldn't speak for the women in the caves.

As she was coming up, she met a lot of women who, married

or single, put their horse before any man or thing. You don't find many men longing for a life of solitary bliss in a single room above a stable, near enough to hear the soft stomping and blowing in the night. They don't place ads. The ads Annie read were full of this dream: "Reliable 30-yr-old wants job as horse-trainer or assistant. Worked as wrangler on dude ranch. Very good with animals. Kathy." "Position wanted by 32-yr-old female, has special way with horses. Connie." "Young woman seeks job on Pennsylvania horse farm. Some experience with training, breaking, breeding. Suzy." "Jockey seeks employment. Works well with horses. 5'3" 105 lbs. Ruth." "Dependable lady seeks live-in position on horse farm. Heavy Walker experience. Julie." "Wanted: job working as horse-trainer on horse ranch or in film industry. Have ability and desire. Lola."

The woman who sold Annie her first horse kept a scrap of newspaper in her wallet—the ad for the first horse she ever bought, her good-luck day, she said. "For sale: Three-year-old blue roan Appaloosa filly. Green broke. Out of Powdered Sugar by Chain Lightning."

Women are the horses' chief protector. The horses' main predators are semis, barbed wire, and men. Not long ago, when cattlemen in helicopters were shooting the last remaining wild horses on the Western range, Mustang Annie and her band of women shot those helicopters out of the sky, from horseback. Now there are protective laws, but men find ways around them. You can lease the public range, but you don't own the water. Still, they surround the free waterholes with barbed wire so the mustangs die of thirst, if they don't get caught in the wire first.

Annie knew what barbed wire does, and not from reading a book. Her mare was the color of root beer, her coat rubbed shiny with flannel. She smelled of pine sap, saddlesoap, and sweet oats. Take this memory and squeeze it to see what else comes out. It wouldn't be so tender if it didn't already have the death in it. Once the horses were chasing each other, galloping hard in big loops around the pasture, feeling wild and happy with the sharp fall air. The mare turned too wide. She crashed through the old barbed wire fence and hung like a fly in a web, streaming the red-dest blood.

Girl children should be born with the strength of ten men and a pair of pliers. After her father cut the mare loose, Annie crept to her bed, hidden things torn and gushing in her stomach, dazed by the fact of her own lack of effect. So helpless. Then she knew why they say "looking at me like a dumb animal" about someone gone beyond reach.

The horse in general is a healthy animal. Though very excit-able to treat. Annie sprang back. She put her faith in practical magic. A half-teaspoon of eucalyptus oil can be mixed with a tablespoon of stiff honey and smeared over a horse's tongue, three times daily, for long life.

To ward off bot-worm, get old sump oil from a garage and ap-ply it to the horse's coat with a rag. This comes from the Spanish gypsies. The Romany gypsies make their horses a cordial ball for strong hearts out of anise seeds, ginger, caraway, and treacle. For epilepsy, give a twice daily drenching with strong skullcap tea. The best medicine is to let them take their own cures by grazing along the side of the road (if it hasn't been sprayed) all over the countryside. Fenced-in grass doesn't have the herbs. Horses need to wander. But if you want your wandering horse to return each night, take seven hairs from your horse's tail and seven from your head. Weave them together with blue thread and a vine of pen-nyroyal, in bloom. Loop it, nail it above the stable door. To bind the two of you even closer, rub the horse's chestnut. This is the rare bone that pierces the skin on the inner foreleg. Humans have nothing comparable. A few flakes will come off in your fingers. Rub them into your palms. Now she will never forget you, you smell like her. You should get in the habit of doing this whenever you groom, to make the spell stronger.

All of Annie's charms worked. Her horses lived long lives and always returned from wandering (although sometimes not before her father had to get her out of school to come home and call them back from trampling the Millers' bean fields. They always came to her call, and only hers.) Charms, however, held no sway over time and the necessity of leaving things behind.

Much later, when she was living in downstate Michigan, the craving overcame her. She got a job leading trail-rides at a place called Seven Oaks. She was out on the trails one day, just a regular customer, when one of the group lost control of his horse. The boy was riding like a cowboy for his girlfriend's benefit: jerks and kicks. He'd gotten the horse Annie wanted in the first place—a black half-Arab named Satan. Satan wouldn't haul that boy up the ravine; he twirled and flipped him ass-first into an ant-hill. So Annie offered to trade. When they all rode back into the yard, the girl who was leading that day called out to the owner, "She rode Satan and he was calm as milk." The owner, George Penny, offered Annie a sort of no-pay job. Lead trail-rides on Sunday and she could come out anytime and ride the black horse. He needed exercise; they had him penned in a stall all day because he scared the shit out of most people.

Annie rode him straight through the winter every day, skip-ping school, everything. George Penny ordered special shoes for him that could go on ice, from England. Sometimes Satan would be so het-up he'd fight her and threaten to go over backwards. Then she'd take him to the track when the sulkies were gone home and let him run his heart out, just cling to his back like a burdock.

She wanted him.

She thought he should be hers.

Annie remembered a tinker's charm: If you paint a certain set of crescent symbols on the hooves with hair oil, then rub salt over it, then whisper certain things in his ear, he belongs to you and no one can come between.

She didn't think about greed or consequence. She painted and salted him on the first full moon. That very week George and Cynthia Penny decided to sell out and move to Arizona. They of-fered her Satan for practically nothing. But his keep would have cost more than what Annie paid for rent. She had no follow-through. They sold him to a farmer near Pinckney. Then they called to say the farmer's son had Satan strapped in a standing martingale and was beating him because Satan wouldn't let the guy on his back. They said they'd get him back if Annie would buy him. She didn't have a cent. That's when she hatched a plan to steal him. The shack Annie rented had been a milk barn and was part of a farm called Hell Creek Ranch. At the time this didn't seem like a joke, it seemed like a sign; he was meant to be hers. The ranch backed up on forty acres of state land, mostly sassafras thicket, and the Crooked River. The river connected Crooked Lake to Half-Moon Lake, where the Pinckney farmer lived.

Annie got a trail map from the ranger station at Crooked Lake. She figured to steal Satan, ride him through the woods following the river to her milk barn house, then trailer him south at night to Indiana, where her cousin had a farm.

It never would have worked, of course. The night before her grand plan was to go into action, Cynthia Penny called once more. She said she and George couldn't stand it, either. They'd bought Satan back themselves. They were going to take him on to Arizona, try to breed him. They thought Annie would want to know he was home safe.

She has not tried to put her mark on anything or anybody since.

Sometimes she wakes, and the pony and mare she had as a child have been staring at her, sadly, over an empty trough. She thinks: God. I forgot to water them and it's been twenty years!

Or if there is lightning, she dreams that the corrugated roof has been hit and barn, fence posts, stile, blackthorns, pony, horse, all have turned into a white ash silhouette.

There was a girl in high school who Annie never liked but did feel a certain bond with because her white mare had been blinded by heat lightning. Annie didn't know if that could be true, but they all believed it. The mare's eyes turned as milky as her coat. The girl could still ride her but had to tap her shoulder before they came to anything taller than a railroad tie, so the mare would lift her foot higher.

You can't be surprised when things happen. You can't go out

of your head when you see a bad storm coming. Annie was wary. The barn was metal, the new fence was electric. They were coralled by lightning.

The only time the mare hurt Annie it was an accident of electricity. She was trying to get the mare in the pasture before a storm. In the furious rain, Annie couldn't see and grabbed bare metal instead of rubber-coated latch. They were both soaked. The current shot through Annie's body and into the mare's head where Annie held her halter. The mare went straight up, then came down full on Annie's foot. She could walk again in a day or two, but the mare was scared of thunder and lightning from then on. She'd cower and shake, as drenched by sweat as if she'd been out in it. The pony and Annie huddled on either side to try to calm her.

In a dream, Annie is alone in Ohio. The grass is long, the horses are still there. The pony gets loose and the mare describes to Annie how he does it. He listens for the hum in the wire. Then he bites off some grass and drops it on the fence. If it touches the wire and the ground, the hum stops. Then he just leans on the dead wire until it snaps. The mare didn't need to give out his secret, Annie had seen him short out the fence a million times.

In another dream, a man Annie loves is riding the mare too hard, impervious to the pain caused to her sensitive mouth. Annie takes the mare from him, cools her down, croons to her, but the spirit is gone from both of them. The man has ruined the thing she held most dear.

Or she dreams that a woman she loves pulls up with a twenty-horse trailer hitched to her truck. It's an antique low wooden traveling horse-house with blue shutters over spacious windows. Annie and the woman are going to convert it to two apartments and live there with the one remaining horse—a majestic palomino.

Then there's the one where loose horses of all ages gambol and bump her under a dawn sky lightening to apricot. Her mother is exercising horses in a ring, all without saddles or bridles, free. A little difficult if one of them decides to lie down, she thinks.

What do you tug on to get it to keep going? Annie realizes she is in her socks. Unshod.

The dream horses are her telepathic rein. They appear at the points of powerlessness—starved, curbed. At the moments of self-initiated actions—vital. They tell her not to forget them. They tell her to choose love without obligation or restriction.

A White Heron

SARAH ORNE JEWETT

I.

*T*he woods were already filled with shadows one June evening, just before eight o'clock, though a bright sunset still glim-
mered faintly among the trunks of the trees. A little girl was driving home her cow, a plodding, dilatory, provoking creature in her
behavior, but a valued companion for all that. They were going
away from the western light, and striking deep into the dark
woods, but their feet were familiar with the path, and it was no
matter whether their eyes could see it or not.

There was hardly a night the summer through when the old
cow could be found waiting at the pasture bars; on the contrary,
it was her greatest pleasure to hide herself away among the high
huckleberry bushes, and though she wore a loud bell she had
made the discovery that if one stood perfectly still it would not
ring. So Sylvia had to hunt for her until she found her, and call
Co'! Co'! with never an answering Moo, until her childish patience was quite spent. If the creature had not given good milk

and plenty of it, the case would have seemed very different to her owners. Besides, Sylvia had all the time there was, and very little use to make of it. Sometimes in pleasant weather it was a consola- tion to look upon the cow's pranks as an intelligent attempt to play hide and seek, and as the child had no playmates she lent herself to this amusement with a good deal of zest. Though this chase had been so long that the wary animal herself had given an unusual signal of her whereabouts, Sylvia had only laughed when she came upon Mistress Moolly at the swamp-side, and urged her affectionately homeward with a twig of birch leaves. The old cow was not inclined to wander farther, she even turned in the right direction for once as they left the pasture, and stepped along the road at a good pace. She was quite ready to be milked now, and seldom stopped to browse. Sylvia wondered what her grandmother would say because they were so late. It was a great while since she had left home at half past five o'clock, but every- body knew the difficulty of making this errand a short one. Mrs. Tilley had chased the hornéd torment too many summer evenings herself to blame any one else for lingering, and was only thankful as she waited that she had Sylvia, nowadays, to give such valuable assistance. The good woman suspected that Sylvia loi- tered occasionally on her own account; there never was such a child for straying about out-of-doors since the world was made! Everybody said that it was a good change for a little maid who had tried to grow for eight years in a crowded manufacturing town, but, as for Sylvia herself, it seemed as if she never had been alive at all before she came to live at the farm. She thought often with wistful compassion of a wretched dry geranium that be- longed to a town neighbor.

" 'Afraid of folks,' " old Mrs. Tilley said to herself, with a smile, after she had made the unlikely choice of Sylvia from her daughter's houseful of children, and was returning to the farm. " 'Afraid of folks,' they said! I guess she won't be troubled no great with 'em up to the old place!" When they reached the door of the lonely house and stopped to unlock it, and the cat came to purr loudly, and rub against them, a deserted pussy, indeed, but fat with young robins, Sylvia whispered that this was a beautiful place to live in, and she never should wish to go home.

The comapnions followed the shady woodroad, the cow taking slow steps, and the child very fast ones. The cow stopped long at the brook to drink, as if the pasture were not half a swamp, and Sylvia stood still and waited, letting her bare feet cool themselves in the shoal water, while the great twilight moths struck softly against her. She waded on through the brook as the cow moved away, and listened to the thrushes with a heart that beat fast with pleasure. There was a stirring in the great boughs overhead. They were full of little birds and beasts that seemed to be wideawake, and going about their world, or else saying goodnight to each other in sleepy twitters. Sylvia herself felt sleepy as she walked along. However, it was not much farther to the house, and the air was soft and sweet. She was not often in the woods so late as this, and it made her feel as if she were a part of the gray shadows and the moving leaves. She was just thinking how long it seemed since she first came to the farm a year ago, and wondering if everything went on in the noisy town just the same as when she was there; the thought of the great red-faced boy who used to chase and frighten her made her hurry along the path to escape from the shadow of the trees.

Suddenly this little woods-girl is horror-stricken to hear a clear whistle not very far away. Not a bird's whistle, which would have a sort of friendliness, but a boy's whistle, determined, and somewhat aggressive. Sylvia left the cow to whatever sad fate might await her, and stepped discreetly aside into the bushes, but she was just too late. The enemy had discovered her, and called out in a very cheerful and persuasive tone, "Halloa, little girl, how far is it to the road?" and trembling Sylvia answered almost inaudiably, "A good ways."

She did not dare to look boldly at the tall young man, who carried a gun over his shoulder, but she came out of her bush and again followed the cow, while he walked alongside.

"I have been hunting for some birds," the stranger said kindly, "and I have lost my way, and need a friend very much. Don't be afraid," he added gallantly. "Speak up and tell me what your name is, and whether you think I can spend the night at your house, and go out gunning early in the morning."

Sylvia was more alarmed than before. Would not her grand-mother consider her much to blame? But who could have foreseen such an accident as this? It did not appear to be her fault, and she hung her head as if the stem of it were broken, but managed to answer "Sylvy," with much effort when her companion again asked her name.

Mrs. Tilley was standing in the doorway when the trio came into view. The cow gave a loud moo by way of explanation.

"Yes, you'd better speak up for yourself, you old trial! Where'd she tuck herself away this time, Sylvy?" Sylvia kept an awed silence; she knew by instinct that her grandmother did not comprehend the gravity of the situation. She must be mistaking the stranger for one of the farmer-lads of the region.

The young man stood his gun beside the door, and dropped a heavy game-bag beside it; then he bade Mrs. Tilley good-evening, and repeated his wayfarer's story, and asked if he could have a night's lodging.

"Put me anywhere you like," he said. "I must be off early in the morning, before day; but I am very hungry, indeed. You can give me some milk at any rate, that's plain."

"Dear sakes, yes," responded the hostess, whose long slum-bering hospitality seemed to be easily awakened. "You might fare better if you went out on the main road a mile or so, but you're welcome to what we've got. I'll milk right off, and you make your-self at home. You can sleep on husks or feathers," she proffered graciously. "I raised them all myself. There's good pasturing for geese just below here towards the ma'sh. Now step round and set a plate for the gentleman, Sylvy!" And Sylvia promptly stepped. She was glad to have something to do, and she was hungry herself.

It was a surprise to find so clean and comfortable a little

dwelling in this New England wilderness. The young man had known the horrors of its most primitive housekeeping, and the dreary squalor of that level of society which does not rebel at the companionship of hens. This was the best thrift of an old-fashioned farmstead, though on such a small scale that it seemed like a hermitage. He listened eagerly to the old woman's quaint talk, he watched Sylvia's pale face and shining gray eyes with ever growing enthusiasm, and insisted that this was the best supper he had eaten for a month; then, afterward, the new-made friends sat down in the doorway together while the moon came up.

Soon it would be berry-time, and Sylvia was a great help at picking. The cow was a good milker, though a plaguy thing to keep track of, the hostess gossiped frankly, adding presently that she had buried four children, so that Sylvia's mother, and a son (who might be dead) in California were all the children she had left. "Dan, my boy, was a great hand to go gunning," she explained sadly. "I never wanted for pa'tridges or gray squer'ls while he was to home. He's been a great wand'rer, I expect, and he's no hand to write letters. There, I don't blame him, I'd ha' seen the world myself if it had been so I could.

"Sylvia takes after him," the grandmother continued affectionately, after a minute's pause. "There ain't a foot o' ground she don't know her way over, and the wild creatur's counts her one o' themselves. Squer'ls she'll tame to come an' feed right out o' her hands, and all sorts o' birds. Last winter she got the jay-birds to bangeing here, and I believe she'd 'a' scanted herself of her own meals to have plenty to throw out amongst 'em, if I hadn't kep' watch. Anything but crows, I tell her, I'm willin' to help support,—though Dan he went an' tamed one o' them that did seem to have reason same as folks. It was round here a good spell after he went away. Dan an' his father they didn't hitch,—but he never held up his head ag'in after Dan had dared him an' gone off."

The guest did not notice this hint of family sorrows in his eager interest in something else.

"So Sylvy knows all about birds, does she?" he exclaimed, as he looked round at the little girl who sat, very demure but increasingly sleepy, in the moonlight. "I am making a collection of birds myself. I have been at it ever since I was a boy." (Mrs. Tilley smiled.) "There are two or three very rare ones I have been hunting for these five years. I mean to get them on my own ground if they can be found."

"Do you cage 'em up?" asked Mrs. Tilley doubtfully, in response to this enthusiastic announcement.

"Oh, no, they're stuffed and preserved, dozens and dozens of them," said the ornithologist, "and I have shot or snared every one myself. I caught a glimpse of a white heron three miles from here on Saturday, and I have followed it in this direction. They have never been found in this district at all. The little white heron, it is," and he turned again to look at Sylvia with the hope of discovering that the rare bird was one of her acquaintances.

But Sylvia was watching a hop-toad in the narrow footpath.

"You would know the heron if you saw it," the stranger continued eagerly. "A queer tall white bird with soft feathers and long thin legs. And it would have a nest perhaps in the top of a high tree, made of sticks, something like a hawk's nest."

Sylvia's heart gave a wild beat; she knew that strange white bird, and had once stolen softly near where it stood in some bright green swamp grass, away over at the other side of the woods. There was an open place where the sunshine always seemed strangely yellow and hot, where tall, nodding rushes grew, and her grandmother had warned her that she might sink in the soft black mud underneath and never be heard of more. Not far beyond were the salt marshes and beyond those was the sea, the sea which Sylvia wondered and dreamed about, but never had looked upon, though its great voice could often be heard above the noise of the woods on stormy nights.

"I can't think of anything I should like so much as to find that heron's nest," the handsome stranger was saying. "I would give ten dollars to anybody who could show it to me," he added desperately, "and I mean to spend my whole vacation hunting for it if need be. Perhaps it was only migrating, or had been chased out of its own region by some bird of prey."

Mrs. Tilley gave amazed attention to all this, but Sylvia still watched the toad, not divining, as she might have done at some calmer time, that the creature wished to get to its hole under the doorstep, and was much hindered by the unusual spectators at that hour of the evening. No amount of thought, that night, could decide how many wished-for treasures the ten dollars, so lightly spoken of, would buy.

The next day the young sportsman hovered about the woods, and Sylvia kept him company, having lost her first fear of the friendly lad, who proved to be most kind and sympathetic. He told her many things about the birds and what they knew and where they lived and what they did with themselves. And he gave her a jack-knife, which she thought as great a treasure as if she were a desert-islander. All day long he did not once make her troubled or afraid except when he brought down some unsuspecting singing creature from its bough. Sylvia would have liked him vastly better without his gun; she could not understand why he killed the very birds he seemed to like so much. But as the day waned, Sylvia still watched the young man with loving admiration. She had never seen anybody so charming and delightful; the woman's heart, asleep in the child, was vaguely thrilled by a dream of love. Some premonition of that great power stirred and swayed these young foresters who traversed the solemn woodlands with soft-footed silent care. They stopped to listen to a bird's song; they pressed forward again eagerly, parting the branches,—speaking to each other rarely and in whispers; the young man going first and Sylvia following, fascinated, a few steps behind, with her gray eyes dark with excitement.

She grieved because the longed-for white heron was elusive, but she did not lead the guest, she only followed, and there was no such thing as speaking first. The sound of her own unquestioned voice would have terrified her,—it was hard enough to answer yes or no when there was need of that. At last evening began to fall, and they drove the cow home together, and Sylvia smiled with pleasure when they came to the place where she heard the whistle and was afraid only the night before.

II.

Half a mile from home, at the farther edge of the woods, where the land was highest, a great pine-tree stood, the last of its generation. Whether it was left for a boundary mark, or for what reason, no one could say; the woodchoppers who had felled its mates were dead and gone long ago, and a whole forest of sturdy trees, pines and oaks and maples, had grown again. But the stately head of this old pine towered above them all and made a landmark for sea and shore miles and miles away. Sylvia knew it well. She had always believed that whoever climbed to the top of it could see the ocean; and the little girl had often laid her hand on the great rough trunk and looked up wistfully at those dark boughs that the wind always stirred, no matter how hot and still the air might be below. Now she thought of the tree with a new excitement, for why, if one climbed it at break of day, could not one see all the world, and easily discover whence the white heron flew, and mark the place, and find the hidden nest?

What a spirit of adventure, what wild ambition! What fancied triumph and delight and glory for the later morning when she could make known the secret! It was almost too real and too great for the childish heart to bear.

All night the door of the little house stood open, and the whippoorwills came and sang upon the very step. The young sportsman and his old hostess were sound asleep, but Sylvia's great design kept her broad awake and watching. She forgot to think of sleep. The short summer night seemed as long as the winter darkness, and at last when the whippoorwills ceased, and she was afraid the morning would after all come too soon, she stole out of the house and followed the pasture path through the woods, hastening toward the open ground beyond, listening with a sense of comfort and companionship to the drowsy twitter of a half-awakened bird, whose perch she had jarred in passing. Alas, if the great wave of human interest which flooded for the first time this dull little life should sweep away the satisfactions of an existence heart to heart with nature and the dumb life of the forest!

There was the huge tree asleep yet in the paling moonlight, and small and hopeful Sylvia began with utmost bravery to mount to the top of it, with tingling, eager blood coursing the channels of her whole frame, with her bare feet and fingers, that pinched and held like bird's claws to the monstrous ladder reaching up, up, almost to the sky itself. First she must mount the white oak tree that grew alongside, where she was almost lost among the dark branches and the green leaves heavy and wet with dew; a bird fluttered off its nest, and a red squirrel ran to and fro and scolded pettishly at the harmless housebreaker. Sylvia felt her way easily. She had often climbed there, and knew that higher still one of the oak's upper branches chafed against the pine trunk, just where its lower boughs were set close together. There, when she made the dangerous pass from one tree to the other, the great enterprise would really begin.

She crept out along the swaying oak limb at last, and took the daring step across into the old pine-tree. The way was harder than she thought; she must reach far and hold fast, the sharp dry twigs caught and held her and scratched her like angry talons, the pitch made her thin little fingers clumsy and stiff as she went round and round the tree's great stem, higher and higher upward. The sparrows and robins in the woods below were beginning to wake and twitter to the dawn, yet it seemed much lighter there aloft in the pine-tree, and the child knew that she must hurry if her project were to be of any use.

The tree seemed to lengthen itself out as she went up, and to reach farther and farther upward. It was like a great main-mast to the voyaging earth; it must truly have been amazed that morning through all its ponderous frame as it felt this determined spark of human spirit creeping and climbing from higher branch to branch. Who knows how steadily the least twigs held themselves to advantage this light, weak creature on her way! The old pine must have loved his new dependent. More than all the hawks, and bats, and moths, and even the sweet-voiced thrushes, was the brave, beating heart of the solitary gray-eyed child. And the tree stood still and held away the winds that June morning while the dawn grew bright in the east.

Sylvia's face was like a pale star, if one had seen it from the ground, when the last thorny bough was past, and she stood trembling and tired but wholly triumphant, high in the tree-top. Yes, there was the sea with the dawning sun making a golden dazzle over it, and toward that glorious east flew two hawks with slow-moving pinions. How low they looked in the air from that height when before one had only seen them far up, and dark against the blue sky. Their gray feathers were as soft as moths; they seemed only a little way from the tree, and Sylvia felt as if she too could go flying away among the clouds. Westward, the woodlands and farms reached miles and miles into the distance; here and there were church steeples, and white villages; truly it was a vast and awesome world.

The birds sang louder and louder. At last the sun came up bewilderingly bright. Sylvia could see the white sails of ships out at sea, and the clouds that were purple and rose-colored and yellow at first began to fade away. Where was the white heron's nest in the sea of green branches, and was this wonderful sight and pageant of the world the only reward for having climbed to such a giddy height? Now look down again, Sylvia, where the green marsh is set among the shining birches and dark hemlocks; there where you saw the white heron once you will see him again; look, look! a white spot of him like a single floating feather comes up from the dead hemlock and grows larger, and rises, and comes close at last, and goes by the landmark pine with steady sweep of wing and outstretched slender neck and crested head. And wait! wait! do not move a foot or a finger, little girl, do not send an arrow of light and consciousness from your two eager eyes, for the heron has perched on a pine bough not far beyond yours, and cries back to his mate on the nest, and plumes his feathers for the new day!

The child gives a long sigh a minute later when a company of shouting cat-birds comes also to the tree, and vexed by their flut-tering and lawlessness the solemn heron goes away. She knows his secret now, the wild, light, slender bird that floats and wavers, and goes back like an arrow presently to his home in the green world beneath. Then Sylvia, well satisfied, makes her peri-lous way down again, not daring to look far below the branch she stands on, ready to cry sometimes because her fingers ache and her lamed feet slip. Wondering over and over again what the stranger would say to her, and what he would think when she told him how to find his way straight to the heron's nest.

"Sylvy, Sylvy!" called the busy old grandmother again and again, but nobody answered, and the small husk bed was empty, and Sylvia had disappeared.

The guest waked from a dream, and remembering his day's pleasure hurried to dress himself that it might sooner begin. He was sure from the way the shy little girl looked once or twice yes-terday that she had at least seen the white heron, and now she must really be persuaded to tell. Here she comes now, paler than ever, and her worn old frock is torn and tattered, and smeared with pine pitch. The grandmother and the sportsman stand in the door together and question her, and the splendid moment has come to speak of the dead hemlock-tree by the green marsh.

But Sylvia does not speak after all, though the old grand-mother fretfully rebukes her, and the young man's kind appealing eyes are looking straight in her own. He can make them rich with money; he has promised it, and they are poor now. He is so well worth making happy, and he waits to hear the story she can tell.

No, she must keep silence! What is it that suddenly forbids her and makes her dumb? Has she been nine years growing, and now, when the great world for the first time puts out a hand to her, must she thrust it aside for a bird's sake? The murmur of the pine's green branches is in her ears, she remembers how the white heron came flying through the golden air and how they watched the sea and the morning together, and Sylvia cannot speak; she cannot tell the heron's secret and give its life away.

Dear loyalty, that suffered a sharp pang as the guest went away disappointed later in the day, that could have served and followed him and loved him as a dog loves! Many a night Sylvia heard the echo of his whistle haunting the pasture path as she came home with the loitering cow. She forgot even her sorrow at the sharp report of his gun and the piteous sight of thrushes and sparrows dropping silent to the ground, their songs hushed and their pretty feathers stained and wet with blood. Were the birds better friends than their hunter might have been, — who can tell? Whatever treasures were lost to her, woodlands and summertime, remember! Bring your gifts and graces and tell your secrets to this lonely country child!

The Bear

YVONNE PEPIN

June 17

Fear never squeezed me as hard as it did last night. A rattling, runting, crashing sound under the cabin woke me. "Men," I thought. "Someone is trying to break into the cabin, rob and rape me."

I lay as still as an ice jam in February, hoping that whoever was underneath the cabin would just go away. My mouth turned to hot metal and I shook in constant little spasms. Inipi was outside somewhere, so I had nothing for comfort or protection. Pretty soon I figured the noise must be an animal because it was clumsy sounding. I got out of bed, trying to support myself on weak knees, and jumped up and down on the loft floor, hoping the repercussions would frighten whatever was under the cabin away.

It must have. There was a finale of crashes and then nothing. I lay in bed, my eyes saucers set into my tight face. I really

Excerpted from *Three Summers: A Journal* (Shameless Hussy Press).

wanted a shot of scotch to calm my shaking, but was too afraid that what had been under the cabin was on the porch and would catch sight of me as I passed the downstairs window. So there I lay, flipping around until dawn.

Carefully, and very slowly, at about 6 a.m., when light was just beginning to shoo away the night, I pushed the door open, after making sure the coast was clear. Nothing on the porch, so I walked toward the steps. What I saw was like a segment from a Walt Disney movie.

Brand new garbage cans that had stored my wheat berries, corn and soy beans had been carried up the hill and emptied. Teeth marks pierced the aluminum cans and the tops were squished. Grains sprinkled the hillside. A white, five-gallon bucket full of powdered milk looked like a colander. A 60-pound metal container of honey was ripped apart like a soup can hit by a shotgun.

Chaos under the cabin . . . clothes strewn about, trampled in the ground, tools knocked from their holdings, and every box turned over and investigated. Unadulterated fear ran through me like the reaction in a fluorescent tube before the milky light announces its compatibility with other gasses.

I started up the hill to analyze the mess. Places in the earth were rooted up and patches of dirt revealed paw prints. I decided whatever had made off with my food might be lurking about, ready for dessert. I ran back into the cabin, built a fire, hoping the smoke would scare the mysterious intruder deeper into the forest where it belonged. My Animals of the Northwest book identified the print I'd seen as bear. I made a strong cup of coffee, or really half coffee and half scotch, and thought about making a run for the truck and dashing into town with a report of a bear attack. Maybe the fish and game man would come and rescue me. Instead I ran down the hill, jumped in the truck, slamming the door and pushing down the lock, and blew the horn on and off for about five minutes. If the fire didn't smoke the varmint out perhaps the horn would blast him, or at least inform a neighbor of the seriousness of my plight; doubtful though, since the nearest neighbor was three miles down the mountain.

When the sun was bright on the steps, about 9 a.m., I ventured out of the cabin. I tied a cow bell around my waist and, armed with the iron fire poker, one of my brother's ferrier products, I made for the outhouse up the hill through the mess. Over 150 dollars' worth of supplies in the bellies of bears.

I didn't stray far from the cabin the rest of the day and cautiously cleaned up the devastation, always alert to any noise or movement. Fear, and anticipation of another bear visit, had me honed sharp.

June 26

Paralysis overcame me last night as I sat reading before the fire: a sodden clomp-clomp on the porch announced an unexpected visitor. When I could bring my head to look up from the page I came face to face with a bear looking in the window. It stood on its back legs, only a thin pane of glass between us. I grabbed the fire poker and ran up into the loft, pulling the ladder up behind me.

The bear must have been as frightened of me as I was of him because I heard him dash off the porch. I waited awhile, went quickly back down to extinguish the lamp, then back up again. I kept the ladder upstairs all night and slept badly, thinking the bear would be back any minute.

July 9

The bear or bears were back last night. They didn't get what little food I had left, but they did clamber about on the porch. I discovered claw marks on the board nailed over the window.

This morning I slept a little later than usual, 7 a.m., because I was awake so much in the night with hearing all the commotion on the porch. I feel more rested, and consequently happier and more centered. I wrote until afternoon outside on the porch steps, had a good bucket and creek bath, dried in the sun, ate lunch and then got around to working on the studio.

Unsuccessfully I played chainsaw mechanic, but gave up and

cut trees and brush around the building site with an axe instead. I worked until evening, went back to the cabin, had a little supper by the creek, and dessert of laced coffee on the porch. After evening chores, water hauled, wood split, lamps filled, wicks trimmed, globes shined, I went back down and dug some more on the studio cellar. Tonight my ovaries ache, perhaps from draw-knifing or lifting too many logs, digging, I don't know what. I haven't seen any bear today, but will keep a fire going all night, thinking the smoke will scare them away.

July 12

I stood on the porch and felt the day's work in my bones, saw the day's work completed . . . the bathtub installed over a shallow pit near the creek, eight logs drawknifed, and a shelf built beside the stove. I feel the value of my home through my bones, in my heart a peaceful fullness.

I've been reading a lot of academic philosophy lately and have concluded that intellectualism is a deviation from innate feelings, the aftermath being an abstract reality that one's mind must conform to. It's all in one's mind, the power to alter reality. I tell myself this lately, often in the face of fear. An experience doesn't have to be frightening unless I will it. At times my will is influenced by ignorance, like with the bears. Since I only know about bears from mythical storybooks, true life adventures in hunting magazines, and Disney nature films, my perceptions of the animal are tainted by others' experiences.

I ran smack into a bear cub this afternoon. On my way to the outhouse we just crossed each other's path. I could have reached out and petted him. In fact, this was my initial response, he looked so cute and cuddly. I knew better though. One thing I learned from a Disney film that altered my perceptions of this afternoon's situation was: don't play with a cub because the mama should be close by. She was. I saw her lumber across the creek and up the hill as I ran to the cabin and slammed the door behind me.

July 22

I asked the fish and game warden if he would come and live-trap the bears. The grumpy man, trying to conceal the boredom of his desk job with an air of power, said they couldn't afford to do that kind of thing. He did promise though he would send some men with dogs up my way to chase the bear into another area. Once a dog has trailed a bear, the bear won't come back, he said.

I made the warden promise not to shoot the bear. I'm feeling very protective of them lately, despite my fears and frustrations. Every time I tell someone in town, usually men, they all want to come up with their high-powered super-duper rifles and get the "mothers." I'm sure these men only see the machismo prestige of using their fancy weapons and a bear skin on their wall. These men get a wild, malicious look on their faces, so now I keep quiet. Word spreads fast though. Last Sunday two guys drove their truck right to the foot of the porch, said they heard I'd been having trouble with bear and could they hunt on my property.

When I turned them around with my words, saying I would rather find ways to live with the bear than resort to killing them, they scowled at me, and reluctantly drove off. Later that evening, when I walked down to watch the sunset, I saw a pile of beer cans, cigarette packages and candy-bar wrappers along the road.

If I had my way I would hunt these men and get six women, each with a pot of honey, to lead a dance of bears over the mountain range.

July 23

Each day my awareness of how men suppress their feelings deepens as I ignore my own. My continual urge to cry lately I attribute to my waxing menstrual cycle. I know though that I'm lonely, tired, and need some gentle understanding of what I've been through this summer. If I don't keep deadening my vulnerability I'll start blubbering, and there is no one to cuddle me.

The grey-muzzled bear was back this afternoon in broad daylight. Down at the fuel shed, with a full lamp, I saw the cub. I turned to retreat into the shed when a grunt on my left pulled my attention. It was the gray-muzzled bear and it reared up on its hind legs. I dropped the lamp and shut the shed door. Locked inside with kerosene, gas and oil cans, I knew I would have to kill a bear. Since it was my karma I had to take it in my own hands.

I drove down to Dave's and explained the situation. He showed me how to use his gun out back by the corral he uses to load pigs and cattle into his truck.

Down the road about 200 yards he set a stump. Dave pushed a shell, which I call a bullet, into the magazine, which I called the chamber. He showed me how to line up the little bead at the end of the sight, pull the trigger and eject the shell.

He gave me the gun and said to steady the barrel on the fence post. I did, and shot. The rifle kicked my shoulder, the noise rang my ears in disbelief. The stump blew in two.

"Why you little fart," Dave said.

I was shaking, nerves and excitement, not fear. I wasn't afraid of the rifle, but it was such a new, violent sensation.

"Try again, sweetheart," he said.

I hesitated. Dave sensed my trepidation with the gun.

"Want me to come up and get the bugger for ya honey?" he said kindly.

I aimed and fired. A direct hit. The stump was pulp.

"You little fart," Dave whispered loudly. "You can do it."

I drove home with the rifle behind the seat, my ears still ringing from the shot, not sure of using the gun, especially to kill something.

July 25

I'm rocking myself in the rocker, wishing I were four years old again with pneumonia, in my mother's lap. In my lap is a loaded 30-30, a damp, blood-stained bear bone in my pocket. I'm estranged, hollow, at the same time filled with grief beyond what I felt from the deaths of my father and mother. It is a grief that culminates beyond the loss and mourning of death. What I feel now is death from killing, a more soul-searching loss, in my own

hands. The left holds death . . . the right, murder. My heart contains pitying remorse.

It began this morning: another episode in my one mountain
woman's life of doing something I've never done before and taking
the brunt of my actions because I am the only one available for
duty. I do what I do out of intelligence or ignorance, depending
on my grounding in the matter.

It began as a typical day; morning coffee, my bath, lunch by
the creek, as normal as any day that has been lived with regularity, including another encounter with a bear. Today, though,
unlike the others, I decided to shoot one.

On the path to the creek I met the cub again. This time, instead of running for shelter, I ran to my shelter for my weapon.
Thoughts and action had no separation and cranked through me
like a reel in fast motion. I waited for the mama bear to find her
cub. My actions were deliberate. I was not in any immediate
danger. The only danger was in my mind, what I imagined the
mother bear would do to me if I got between her and her cub.

Grey-muzzle came sauntering, unaware of my post on the
porch, out of some bushes near the creek. I steadied the barrel on
the porch rail, spread my legs, and got him/her in my sight. Just
when I believed I could pull the trigger, old grey-muzzle turned
and walked back in the undergrowth. I wouldn't shoot unless it
was going to be accurate.

I waited some more, wearing only shorts, the costume of an
Indian brave, though I didn't feel so brave. Twenty minutes
passed and a few minutes later another bear came out of the same
spot in the bushes.

The bear walked across the creek, stopped in the middle,
about 300 yards away. I aimed, its chest covered by my bead, my
mouth like ash, my limbs pudding. Composure—like when I'm
putting the finishing touches on an oil painting with a triple-O
sable brush—elbows pressed to my sides, I hold my breath, then
apply the stroke.

A slowly squeezed trigger, a fast shot, no time between action and impact—a look of surprise. The bear's front legs flew out of the water, its eye made contact with mine. A look of disbelief. Clumsily it splashed forward in the water, all in less than a second. It turned and ran into the bushes from where it had come. I fired again and again.

I was in shock. This was real now. I shook so hard I decided not to lace up my shoes and just took after the wounded animal. Bushes rustled, I ran back to the cabin. A wounded bear, I'd heard, is vicious; they will play dead, then attack.

I flew down the road in the truck, not closing any gates, to call the game warden. At the neighbors' I babbled intensely about the bear, the shot, the wounded bear. "I have to call the warden to come and kill it." On the line the warden says it's all in my hands.

The neighbors say they will help. Dave, whose house I called from, calls Bill. Bill gets two of his sons and their dog. They load into my little truck. A macho procession—men, guns, dogs.

At the cabin I lead the men to where I shot the bear. Bill scouts around, finds a bloody bone chip on a rock in the creek, more blood on some branches and grass leading up the creek.

"Looks like a rib bone," he says. "He won't get far."

I take the bone, roll it between my fingers, not believing it is true, and pocket it. We pair off, the boys go upstream, I go downstream with Dave, Bill and the dog, an old, swaybacked, whiskered thing that has run cattle five years too long.

The men say a wounded animal will stay near water, but the dog, who has smelled a bearblooded stick, leads us up into the rocks. By this time I'm exhausted and beginning to feel overwhelming sadness, but the intensity of the hunt sends adrenalin into my veins.

We search the woods for over an hour. I have to pee so bad I can hardly keep up with the men, but am too embarrassed and afraid to go in the bushes. The dog is really no help. We try to think like a bear. If I had my rib bone shot out where would I go? Probably to my home. Where do bears live? In caves? We searched the rocks. No signs. I fingered the bone chip in my pocket.

Everyone rendezvoused at the cabin. We all had stories to tell, no bear to show. I drew a bucket of water and passed around cups. We all drank heavily.

Talk was of my shot—it impressed them all; over 300 yards and in the chest at that. The men said the bear should be dead by now, or bleed to death by tomorrow, with the heat and all infecting the wound. The men say the bear has most likely gone into the rocks. "Watch for vultures," they say. The black, circling birds indicate a wounded or dying animal.

When I drove the men back down the mountain they all wanted me to spend the night at their house; in fact, their wives were the ones to suggest it. The women said I was brave. I felt disgusted with myself. Bravery is not using a gun with the intent to kill. Funny, too, how the men's attitude toward me changed. I felt like one of the "guys." On the porch after the chase, Dave, who always refers to me as honey, sweetheart or girlie, said, "This woman sure knows how to use a gun."

The full impact of this afternoon comes booming into me tonight. I have committed an act so contrary to my nature and the philosophy I seek to uphold on this land—coexistence. I've killed a part of my belief today, that I can live in harmony with nature, at ease with what she dishes out.

I have not eaten meat for six years because I didn't want the responsibility of killing. Now I have killed, and it was not for food, but because of fear. I've killed an animal, more a native to this mountain saddle than myself. I tell myself it was a matter of survival for the fittest.

Technology has made me God.

Tonight, every shape is a bear, every snapping twig or whoosh of branch is the bear, come back to retaliate, seek revenge . . . karma. I allow myself only a little wine, knowing I need to keep sharp. But I need something to take me away from this consuming pit of anguish.

July 26

My vocabulary of loneliness has expanded. It has nothing to do with feeling unattached from others or oneself. A loneliness, not from loss, but from action, accountability. Just as I have created beautiful experiences living here, I've brought into my awareness now morbidity, grief, sorrow.

Death is in the air. The trees with their ghostly rushes of branch and air are shaming me. A dipping bird lighted for a moment on the rock in the stream and flew away as if spooked by the unseen, the rock where I picked up the bloody bear bone I still fondle in my pocket.

A day of mourning prevails. The furthest I stray from the cabin is to the outhouse, and then armed, expectant, my eyes keen for circling vultures. Nerves stuffed with fear, with anxiety. Just a leaf in my journal, ruffling in the breeze, sends me jumping.

The bear were back last night, as if to say, "Ha, ha!" They tore down my food cache strung in a fir near where I shot the bear. The mess is an old story.

July 27

The familiar, fear-instilling clomp on the porch. Scratching noises on the window molding. Stiff in my bed I listened, hoping the bear would go away. It didn't. I began my bear-scare dance on the floor, banging on the waste basket in time to my loud steps. The bear left.

Within an hour the bear was back. I stuck the rifle out the window, barrel to the stars, and pierced the night with gun powder combusting. A quick scuffle on the porch, bushes rustle, I watch the bear retreat down the path. I hang my head out the loft window, a princess in distress.

My sleep was a roller coaster of dreams, rising and plunging. I couldn't scream in this unconscious state. My mouth formed the expression but remained bound in the silence of sleep. I was walking in the forest, carrying the rifle. A deer crossed my path. I felt a clean, excited rush; the anticipation of killing. The deer fell to the deadening crack of my rifle.

Now I understand what my brother said to me when he told me the story of a deer he had poached. "Why?" I asked.

"There was just this overwhelming feeling," he said, "a rush of blood to my head and I had to shoot it. Oh, forget it, you wouldn't understand."

And I thought he was sick. Now I understand–what it is to respond to the wild, an unsuspecting animal surprised by the devastating blast of a gun–the adrenalin rush in knowing your supremacy; a demented sensation of power, demented because it is all outside of yourself.

While digging out the cellar today, I realized why I compare myself so much to men lately. It's because I don't know any other women who are doing what I'm doing; living alone and working alone in a traditionally male world.

No matter how much more stamina and willpower I have, my physical strength can't compare to most men. Sometimes what takes me an hour of pure struggle, lifting logs for instance, a man can do in 20 minutes. But I work to my full capacity and then beyond.

I know women who accept the fact that they are physically weaker than men and ride through life as passive observers. They let themselves be carried by men over situations, never really demanding of their bodies, strengthening their dependence on men.

A woman living through a man's "privilege," which is also a man's greatest pain, is denying herself access to her masculine side, which in turn over-amps a male's dominant side, and we have unbalanced persons, either too yin or too yang.

July 29

The moon hangs, an illuminated crescent above the mountain. By 5 a.m. the east is beginning to redden and the distant motor of a truck whines closer to the cabin. Two men park below the cabin, a truck bed full of yapping dogs in their wake.

I greet the men on the porch, Bruce Wells and Charlie Pierce.

No time for coffee. When one is tracking bear it must be done while dew is still in the prints. The men had come up the night before, hearing in town that I'd been having bear problems, asking if they could help.

Bruce, a tall lanky man in his early forties, has brown teeth like many of the men out here who chew. He raises "Bear Dogs," which, he says, "I wouldn't trade for a farm in Texas." The dogs look underfed and mean. One of them wears a sharply spiked collar.

Charlie is cute, small for a man, a logger with a limp like Chester on the westerns. Charlie's deformity came last year when a tree fell across his leg; he's been out of work since.

We headed up the creek, Bruce holding the yipping dog pack straining on leashes. He would cuff them hard with the ball of his hand until they quieted down. "It's the only language they understand," he said.

Everybody's eyes point towards the ground. The men said you can tell how old a track is by the dew in it. The direction of the toes, if they point up or down, indicate the rate the bear is traveling. Bruce spotted one dewy paw print and unleashed one dog to blaze a trail.

The dog led us to a torn-up deer. Bloody bones, some still with pink meat and fur on them, lay haphazardly among fallen branches. All the dogs started barking in shrill, unsynchronized rhythm. Bruce cuffed them silent.

A deer kill, the men said, probably brought down by a coyote and the bears fed on the left-overs, then sauntered down the creek to my cabin for dessert.

Bruce poked at a dark pile near a chewed skull and disassembled spinal column. "Bear scat," he said, and dissected ants and bark with a stick from the scat. Bears grub up stumps for a dinner of ants and beetles, and what goes in must come out. This is how I came to learn to distinguish a cow pie from a bear turd.

The bones trailed down the embankment to the creek and across. Bears, the men said, usually wash their food before eating it. Bruce picked up a lower leg bone, the hoof still intact, waved it in front of the dogs' noses and unleashed them. They were gone in a frenzy, barking and baying across the creek and up the hillside, with us in trail.

"Won't they get lost?" I asked. Bruce whistled, and the dogs, by now out of sight, came tumbling back to Bruce's command. "How do you know when they find a bear?" I continued.

"They all start yapping in a high-pitched way. All the noise comes from one direction and is pretty constant." From there, Bruce explained, it is a matter of tracing the sound to animals which have in all probability treed a bear. Then you shoot it, or leave it alone. Bruce explained sometimes he just chases bears for the fun of it and to keep his dogs sharp.

The men's strides are twice as long as mine. It is not so easy hurrying up rocky hillsides and jumping over creeks too wide for me to span in one leap. We stop on a high vantage and watch vultures circling. Vultures, not hawks or eagles. Vultures are black and have shaggy wings that tip up. The men continue on. Vultures mark the spot. I return to the cabin all of a sudden very tired, very sad.

On the porch, I painted a picture of the bear from my memory, trying to recreate the look he gave me, that innocent, unbelieving eye of "Why did you do this to me?" I sang a long song to his spirit. The painting is in a circle, spontaneous, and reflects the fear in me, the fierce-gentleness of the animal.

Carpenter ants crawl around in the cabin, on the porch, have made nests in my wood pile. When I shot the bear I upset the cycle of nature. The bear ate the ants, I killed the bear, now there will be more carpenter ants, millions more, and one less bear. The stump the bear grubbed apart to get at the ants, that fell into decay on the forest floor, became rich life-support humus for many other ecological structures.

It was the bear's innate nature that brought him to my food. He was hungry and found an easy meal. Simple as that. If I was hungry I'd have done the same. If I'd come too close to the bear's den he may have killed me. The bear repeatedly crossed into my boundaries, so I offed him. Technology, however, gave me the edge. Survival for the armed. Do my man-made privileges grant me the right to kill?

I remembered back to a night in Mendocino. I had searched the cemetery until dark to find the right iris to paint. I dug it up, placed in in a bleach jug someone had brought flowers in, and brought the iris into the studio. Well into the painting, letting the mystical qualities of its colors and forms guide me, I realized the iris was wilting. I began to cry. The iris was dying and I was killing it. So, at 3 a.m., I drove back to the cemetery and replanted the flower, praying over it, sprinkling water on it.

I had a brain and the iris did not, but I had felt the consciousness of another form of life. We were both living organisms, with cells, limbs and veins. We were both of the earth, lived and breathed the same air, were nourished by the sun, just like the bear and me.

No matter how much I shamed myself or justified my actions, I still felt horrible about killing the bear. The men came back before lunch and said they had found it . . . dead . . . shot in the chest. They left it rotting in the sun. Other animals would take care of it, unless I wanted to skin it.

"No, let's leave it," I said. When they packed up all their dogs, I gave them a cold beer and thanked them. "We had a great time. No need to thank us." When they were far down the mountain and I felt safe they would not return, I walked to where I'd shot the bear, left the rifle at the cabin, I would take my chances, and moaned and bellowed and cried until I lay still, exhausted.

Afternote: Later that summer agents from the fish and game department informed me that a number of bears had been shot with tranquilizing guns in national parks where they had become a problem. The bears were transported to the national wilderness area behind my cabin. Accustomed to humans and human food these bears were led to my cabin first by the smell of a deer kill. Most bears in a truly wild state will shy from humans unless provoked.

I've Finally Been Accepted by A Gorilla

DIAN FOSSEY

*I*ronically enough it was poachers who introduced me to the first group encountered on Mt. Visoke, Group 4. Two Batwa had been hunting for duiker with bows and arrows, and, upon hearing a screaming outbreak from the slopes of Visoke, came to camp to tell me of the gorillas' whereabouts.

I followed the poachers to the group and returned to camp elated upon having contacted gorillas the first day after having established the Karisoke camp. While typing up my field notes that evening I heard chestbeats and gorilla vocalizations from Visoke's slopes just behind my tent. The sounds were approximately a mile from where I had left Group 4 earlier that day. Because gorilla groups ordinarily travel only some 400 yards a day, I realized that this had to be a second Karisoke study group, Group 5.

Excerpted from *Gorillas In The Mist* (Houghton Mifflin).

The next morning I climbed toward the source of the previous evening's vocalizations, picked up the gorillas' trail, and tracked them to a ridge of thick trees high above the tented camp. Upon seeing me, all the animals instantly hid, with the exception of a young juvenile who treed to chestbeat and flamboyantly swing through the branches before leaping with a crash into the foliage below. Instantly I named him Icarus. The other group members, fifteen in all as I was later to learn, retreated about twenty feet farther from where they had been feeding and peeked at me shyly through dense vegetation. However, the imp, Icarus, boldly climbed a tree again either to show off his acrobatic ability or to stare curiously at the first human being he had ever seen munching wild celery stalks.

Within the first half-hour of the contact with Group 5 I realized that there were two silverbacks in the group who maintained protective flank positions around the females and young. The two males were easily located and recognized because of their disharmonic vocalizations. The elder, dominant male gave deep alarm *wraaghs* and was named Beethoven; the younger silverback had higher-pitched calls and was named Bartok. I later identified an older blackback male in the group and couldn't resist naming him Brahms. Four females were also sighted carrying bug-eyed infants of varying ages. One of the adults calmly sat under the tree where Icarus was vigorously displaying. She protectively hugged an infant to her breast and showed some concern at Icarus' antics. I felt certain that she was the mother of the young acrobat because of their strong facial resemblance and his periodic need to go to her for reassurance. For no particular reason I named the female Effie and the bright-eyed infant she clutched to her breast Piper. After nearly an hour's contact, the gorillas began moving off to feed. Since one of my basic rules is never to follow a group when they choose to leave, I also left, though Icarus briefly remained treed amid his batons of branches.

The habituation of Group 5 progressed smoothly because of the regularity of my contacts. I was able to approach the animals to within twenty feet during the first year of the work at

Karisoke. Beethoven was tolerant of the other two adult males, Bartok and Brahms, since he appeared to rely upon them as watchdogs for the protection of the group's females and young. The highest-ranking female, Effie, along with her daughter Piper, about two years old, and Icarus, between five and six years, maintained the closest proximity to Beethoven, who was consistently indulgent and good-natured whenever his offspring tumbled in play around his huge, silvered bulk. The second-highest-ranking female in the group was Marchessa, who seemed apprehensive of Effie, although Marchessa's daughter, Pantsy, about a year and a half old, never hesitated to mingle among Effie's clan to play with Piper and Icarus. Pantsy had been so named because of a chronic asthmalike condition that affected her vocalizations. More often than not, Pantsy's eyes and nose drained severely, but Marchessa never was observed attempting to clean the infant's face. Two of the remaining four adult females in the group were never given names; I was not absolutely certain which was which because of their tendencies to remain obscured in dense vegetation. The other two females, Liza and Idano, were the last individuals of Group 5 to be named once they lost their shyness of me and could be clearly identified.

Icarus enhanced contacts with the group because of his insatiable curiosity and boldness, which often prompted risky displays in all sizes of trees from spindly saplings to sturdy old *Hagenia*. One day while trying out a new routine on a tree limb not solid enough for such antics, the little elf-eared fellow unintentionally crashed to the ground along with the branch from which he had been swinging. The splintering noises had barely died away before the air was filled with the indignant roars and screams of Beethoven and Bartok. The two males bluff-charged toward me with the group's females bringing up the rear as though they all held me responsible for the fall. The animals stopped about ten feet away when they saw Icarus, still intact, climb another tree impervious to the furor he had created. The mischievous imp appeared all angelic innocence, but the two silverbacks remained quite tense. The air was filled with their pungent fear odor.

I released my clammy hold on the vegetation I had clutched, when, much to my dismay, Icarus' sister, Piper, climbed into the broken sapling he had just discarded. The little juvenile began an uncoordinated series of spins, twirls, kicks, and chest pats. She exuded blasé self-importance as the attention of myself and the gorillas' was riveted on her. No high-wire artist ever had such a rapt audience. The glances of the silverbacks darted back and forth between Piper and myself as if they expected me to leap forward and grab her at any moment. When our eyes met, they roared their disapproval. Suddenly, Icarus broke the nervousness building up among the group members. He climbed playfully into Piper's tree and began a chasing game that led them both back to the watchful group. All three silverbacks then released their tension by chest-beating and running through the tall foliage before leading the group uphill and away.

On a slope gorillas always feel more secure when positioned above humans, or even approaching gorillas. I never relished climbing up to a group from directly below, but there were times when the thickness of the vegetation compelled me to do so. I vividly remember one such contact when crawling up to Group 5 and carrying a heavy Nagra tape recorder. Just about twenty feet below the gorillas, who could be heard feeding above, I softly vocalized to make my presence known. I set up the microphone in a nearby tree and stabilized the tape recorder on the ground. A number of curious infants and juveniles climbed into trees above to stare intently down at the unaccustomed equipment. Upon recognizing me, they began playing pretentiously in flimsy *Veronia* saplings. The feeding sounds among the adults, still out of sight farther up the slope, stopped as the youngsters' dare-deviltry spurred them into wilder and noisier acrobatics. Just as expected, the silverbacks instantly led the females, all hysterically screaming, in a bluff-charge to within ten feet. Because of the incredible intensity of the screams, the needle of the modulation meter on the tape recorder went berserk, bouncing far above the proper intake level. I tried to bend down to adjust the machine's volume, but the slightest movement incited renewed charges from the overwrought animals. For-getting all about the microphone, I dramatically whispered to myself, "I'll never get out of this alive!" When the tape ran out I could only stand helplessly by, glancing alternately at the worried silverbacks directly above and the frantically spinning empty sound reel in the machine at my feet. Only when the group eventually climbed out of sight was it possible to turn off the recorder. That night when listening to the tape in the cabin, my theatrical words, sandwiched between two screaming charges, came as a complete surprise and reduced me to gales of laughter, for I had forgotten ever having whispered them during all the excitement.

Months later I analyzed the vocalizations spectrographically and found that the individual differences distinguished when hear-ing silverbacks' *wraaghs* and other calls were also apparent on the sonograms. This leaves little doubt that gorillas can identify one another by hearing vocalizations emitted by others even over great distances.

By 1969, the second year of Karisoke research, the staff and I had not yet totally succeeded in ridding the saddle terrain of cattle, so Group 5 tenaciously clung to Visoke's southeastern slopes, a region of deep ravines surrounded by steep ridges. It was often possible to track the group to the edge of a ridge and find the animals below sunbathing like so many beach bums. On such occa-sions obscured contacts were maintained in order to observe intra-group interaction unaffected by my presence.

On one rare sunny day, contented belch vocalizations were heard coming up from Group 5 secluded in one of their favorite bowls of rich herbaceous foliage. Quietly I crawled to the edge of the ridge and lay hidden in the brush to observe the peaceable family through binoculars. The patriarch, Beethoven, was nested in the center of the sunning circle, a great silver mound about twice the size of the females clustered around him. I could only estimate his weight as in the neighborhood of three hundred and fifty pounds and his age as probably around forty. His silvering ex-tended along his thighs, neck, and shoulders, where it was more grizzled in color than the near-white saddle region of his dorsal surface. Other sexually dimorphic characteristics, in addition to massive size and silvering, were his pronounced sagittal crest and canines, all physical features never seen in female gorillas.

Slowly Beethoven shifted his great bulk, rolled over onto his back, gave a contented sigh, and speculatively regarded his latest offspring, six-month-old Puck. The infant was playfully tadpoling across the stomach of its mother, Effie, wearing a lopsided grin of enjoyment. Gently, Beethoven lifted Puck up by the scruff of the neck to dangle the exuberant baby over his body before casually grooming it. Puck was nearly obscured from sight by the massive hand, which eventually placed the wide-eyed infant back onto Effie's stomach.

That observation of a silverback sire with his offspring was typical of similar scenes throughout the years to be spent with the gorillas. The extraordinary gentleness of the adult male with his young dispels all the King Kong mythology. . . .

Often I am asked about the most rewarding experience I have ever had with gorillas. The question is extremely difficult to answer because each hour with the gorillas provides its own return and satisfaction. The first occasion when I felt I might have crossed an intangible barrier between human and ape occurred about ten months after beginning the research at Karisoke. Peanuts, Group 8's youngest male, was feeding about fifteen feet away when he suddenly stopped and turned to stare directly at me. The expression in his eyes was unfathomable. Spellbound, I returned his gaze—a gaze that seemed to combine elements of inquiry and of acceptance. Peanuts ended this unforgettable moment by sighing deeply, and slowly resumed feeding. Jubilant, I returned to camp and cabled Dr. Leakey I'VE FINALLY BEEN ACCEPTED BY A GORILLA.*

---

*Nine years after Dr. Leakey's death in 1972 I learned that he had carried the cable in his pocket for months, even taking it on a lecture tour to America. I was told that he read it proudly, much as he once spoke to me of Jane Goodall's outstanding success with chimpanzees.

Two years after our exchange of glances, Peanuts became the first gorilla ever to touch me. The day had started out as an ordinary one, if any day working from Karisoke might be considered ordinary. I felt unusually compelled to make this particular day outstanding because the following morning I had to leave for England for a seven-month period to work on my doctorate. Bob Campbell and I had gone out to contact Group 8 on the western-facing Visoke slopes. We found them feeding in the middle of a shallow ravine of densely growing herbaceous vegetation. Along the ridge leading into the ravine grew large *Hagenia* trees that had always served as good lookout spots for scanning the surrounding terrain. Bob and I had just settled down on a comfortable moss-cushioned *Hagenia* tree trunk when Peanuts, wearing his "I want to be entertained" expression, left his feeding group to meander inquisitively toward us. Slowly I left the tree and pretended to munch on vegetation to reassure Peanuts that I meant him no harm.

Peanuts' bright eyes peered at me through a latticework of vegetation as he began his strutting, swaggering approach. Suddenly he was at my side and sat down to watch my "feeding" techniques as if it were my turn to entertain him. When Peanuts seemed bored with the "feeding" routine, I scratched my head, and almost immediately, he began scratching his own. Since he appeared totally relaxed, I lay back in the foliage, slowly extended my hand, palm upward, then rested it on the leaves. After looking intently at my hand, Peanuts stood up and extended his hand to touch his fingers against my own for a brief instant. Thrilled at his own daring, he gave vent to his excitement by a quick chestbeat before going off to rejoin his group. Since that day, the spot has been called *Fasi Ya Mkoni,* "the Place of the Hands." The contact was among the most memorable of my life among the gorillas. . . .

Once, from a hidden position, I watched Digit, about five and a half years old, tumble onto Uncle Bert's lap much like a puppy wanting attention. From a lazy sunning position, Uncle Bert had watched the youngster's approach, then quickly plucked a handful of white everlasting flowers (*Helichrysum*) to whisk back and forth against Digit's face as if trying to tickle the young male. The action evoked loud play chuckles and a big toothy grin from Digit, who rolled against Uncle Bert's body, clutching himself ecstatically before scampering off to playmates more his own size. I had been pleased to note that little Digit had undergone only a brief period of dejection following Whinny's absence and soon had formed close association with other group members, particularly the four young females thought to be his half sisters.

Play, along with sexual behavior, is one of the first activities inhibited by the presence of an observer until the gorillas become fairly well habituated. This is particularly true with play behavior of small infants, whose mothers and fathers are extremely protective during the first two years of their lives. However, Digit and his half sisters were young adults when I first encountered them, thus were seldom guarded in their play activities. The freedom of their play depended to a great extent upon the type of contact I initiated with the group. During obscured contacts, when Group 4 did not know I was observing them, Digit and his young sisters engaged in prolonged wrestling and chasing sessions as far as fifty feet from day-nesting adults. The constant repetition of their actions seemed almost deliberate, simply to provoke a response from their partners. One by one the youngsters would wear themselves out before joining older members of the group for a resting period. During open contacts, when the group members knew I was present, a great part of the immatures' play behavior involved response reactions such as chestbeating, foliage whacking, or strutting. Each individual seemed to be trying to outdo the other in attention-getting actions. Their excitement was contagious and there were many days that I wanted to join in their escapades and could not do so until they lost their apprehension of my presence.

On one occasion, Group 4 were crossing a high grassy slope supporting several rows of giant *Senecio,* the tall one-legged sentries of the alpine zone. Led by Uncle Bert, the five young ones playfully began a square-dance type of game, using the *Senecio* trees as "doh-see-doh" partners. Loping from one tree to the next, each animal extended its arms to grab a trunk for a quick twirl before repeating the same maneuver with the next tree down the line. The gorillas, spilling down the hill, resembled so many black, furry tumbleweeds as their frolic resulted in a big pile-up of bouncing bodies and broken branches. Time and time again, Uncle Bert playfully led the pack back up the slope for another go-around with the splintered tree remnants. . . .

Like human mothers, gorilla mothers show a great variation in the treatment of their offspring. The contrasts were particularly marked between Old Goat and Flossie. Flossie was very casual in the handling, grooming, and support of both of her infants, whereas Old Goat was an exemplary parent.

Seven months old when Simba, Flossie's first baby, disappeared, Tiger was a thriving, strong-minded bundle of constant motion whose most remarkable feature was his long, wavy, reddish-brown head hair that stuck out in unruly curls around his face and hung in ringlets below his neck. His unusual flaming mane could be seen even at long distances, in marked contrast to Old Goat's jet-black body hair. Typical for his age, Tiger had the faint beginnings of a white tail tuft, his eyes were becoming the predominant feature of his face, and he weighed about eleven pounds. He was usually observed within arm reach of Old Goat and had begun traveling regularly on her back rather than in her arms. Tiger's own attempts to move around independently were still clumsy and uncoordinated. Like most gorilla infants around seven months of age, his main sustenance came from suckling. He was able to pluck at vegetation to eat but had not yet acquired the preparatory skills of stripping leaves or wadding vines. Tiger's increased dexterity in these activities was attributed to his intent scrutiny of the feeding methods of the older animals around him. Also, like other gorilla infants, Tiger never tried taking food away from another individual, though his mother often took dung or nonfood items, such as brightly colored flowers, away from him. He, like other free-living gorillas his age, obtained his first bits of food from remnants of vegetation or bark that had fallen onto his mother's lap.

In October 1969, when Flossie's second offspring approached seven months of age, the younger female Maisie, estimated at about nine and a half years, began showing increasing interest in Flossie's baby. Maisie groomed the older female a great deal, in a contrived effort to gain access to her young infant for grooming or cuddling purposes. Flossie, who strongly resembled Maisie, was extremely tolerant toward her; this led me to suspect that strong kinship ties existed between them. Flossie never objected when Maisie carried her infant off for entire day-resting periods to satisfy her maternal inclinations. This is often called "aunt behavior," a term that implies merely an affinitive relationship. Such behavior enables infants to become accustomed to adults other than their mothers and allows nulliparous females—who have not given birth—to gain maternal experience. . . .

With the 1971 emigrations of Bravado, Maisie, and Macho, Digit lost three half sisters, the peers with whom he had played during his transition from a juvenile to a blackback. Now nearly nine years old, he was too old to cavort freely with one-year-old Augustus, forty-month-old Simba, forty-five-month-old Tiger, or five-year-old Papoose; too young to associate closely with Group 4's older females, Old Goat, Flossie, and Petula. Perhaps for these reasons Digit became more strongly attracted to humans than did other young gorillas among the study groups who had siblings and peers.

I received the impression that Digit really looked forward to the daily contacts with Karisoke's observers as a source of entertainment. Eventually he showed that he could tell the difference between males and females by playfully charging and whacking men but behaving almost coyly with women. He was always the first member of Group 4 to come forward to see who had arrived on any particular day. He seemed pleased whenever I brought strangers along and would completely ignore me to investigate any newcomers by smelling or lightly touching their clothing and hair. If I was alone, he often invited play by flopping over on to his back, waving stumpy legs in the air, and looking at me smiling-ly as if to say, "How can you resist me?" At such times, I fear, my scientific detachment dissolved.

Like Puck of Group 5, Digit became fascinated by thermoses, notebooks, gloves, and camera equipment. He always examined, smelled, and handled everything gently, and occasionally even re-turned objects to their owners. His return of these items was not done from any sense of recognition of ownership but only because he did not like the clutter of human belongings around him.

One day I took a small hand mirror to Group 4 and stood it in the foliage where Digit could see it. Without hesitation he ap-proached, lay propped up on his forearms, and sniffed the glass without touching it. As the young blackback viewed his image, his lips pursed, his head cocked quizzically, he gave a long sigh. Digit continued staring calmly at his reflection before reaching behind the glass to "feel" for the body of the figure before him. Finding nothing, he lay quietly gazing at himself for another five minutes before again sighing and moving away. Often I have puz-zled over Digit's acceptance and apparent pleasure when gazing intently at his reflection. It would be presumptive for me to be-lieve that he recognized himself. Perhaps the lack of scent clues informed him of the absence of another gorilla.

The Rwandese Office of Tourism, in an attempt to attract visitors to the Parc des Volcans, asked me for a photograph of a gorilla to use for a poster advertisement. Since I was a guest in their country, I complied with their request, just as several years previously I had provided a number of pictures of the forest and gorillas to the Rwandese postal service to serve as models for the first series of Rwandan stamps featuring the gorillas of the Parc des Volcans. The slide I selected for the tourist office was one of my lovable Digit. Shortly thereafter large color posters of Digit feeding on a piece of wood were scattered throughout Rwanda — in hotels, banks, the park office, the Kigali airport, and in travel bureaus throughout the world. In various languages the poster was captioned "Come and See Me in Rwanda!" I had very mixed feelings on first seeing the posters around Rwanda. Heretofore Digit had been an "unknown," only a young male maturing within his natal group. Suddenly his face was everywhere. I could not help feeling that our privacy was on the verge of being invaded. . . .

The Donkey

MAY SARTON

*J*oanna stood in the prow of the boat that wends its way with mail and passengers from island to island in the Aegean sea, and let the wind blow her hair wild. It seemed hardly believable that she was off on a month's painting holiday at last, after the years and years of waiting for this moment, years of war, years of near starvation, years of such stress and horror that she put them behind her, and held herself now as if she stood in the prow of the ship of time, her whole being drinking in the wind.

It had been hot when she embarked at Piraeus, lugging canvases and easel strapped together as well as her two suitcases. Her father had objected to the bright blue and green striped slacks. "Dear girl, must you look like a gypsy?"

"It's a holiday, Papa! On a holiday one may look like a gypsy!"

The banter covered a difficult moment of parting, for always

Chapter 1 from *Joanna and Ulysses* (W.W. Norton & Co.).

she carried with her anxiety about her father, who was too old to rally as she had done, her father who had lately become as frail as a blade of grass, and whom she cherished with passionate concern as if she could by the intensity of her caring keep death away. Keep death away. Not look back. For a month she was to give herself to joy, to paint, to think, to feel youth, buried so long, rising up in her like sap into the branches of a battered tree.

Joanna had been under twenty when the war was over, and she was thirty now, but she felt much older. For she had had to become a mother not only to her two brothers, but also to her father when she was fifteen and the tragedy (of which they never spoke) took place. Sometimes Joanna imagined that if her father had been willing to talk about it, it might have helped. Instead, he became a finicky old man, a martinet . . . the two boys had escaped his demands, his neurasthenia, and no longer lived at home, but Joanna herself was a prisoner. This holiday alone, this chance to go off by herself and paint for a month was the first she had ever had, and only now, standing in the prow of the boat, alone and free, she realized how tightly the bow was strung, how great her need to recapture the inner person, the real one. She had sometimes managed to get off on a Saturday to paint, but the results were tight and self-conscious as if she felt her father looking over her shoulder. With all his suffering and the darkness in which he had wrapped himself, he was a good, a severe critic, and he did not take her painting seriously. Neither in fact did Joanna herself: she worked in an office all week, and kept the house going; she nursed her father slowly back from the years when he simply lay in bed and refused to get up, to the point where he did go to his office each day. Yet somewhere deep down inside her there was a being who was not the dutiful daughter she had forced herself to become. She felt she had earned a commitment to this being, the painter, for although she had no illusions about the value of what she did, painting could, she felt, become a way of finding out what she really thought about things, where she was now, at thirty. She was lifted up on the expectation of the effort and the joy ahead, a joy so taut she

wished she could cry it aloud like a seagull: "Listen, sky! Listen,
gulls and sea, I am Joanna! Joanna, the painter!" Oh yes, she had
kept her innocence, this Joanna who was no longer young; she
had kept her sense of herself as a wild creature, a person who
could address God or the sky on a man-to-man basis. Let us say,
simply, that she was a Greek, the tall dark woman, standing in
the prow of the shabby boat, exulting.

She had seen one island after another rise up out of the
cerulean blue sea, first a distant hump, then an escarpment of
rocks, sometimes the blond semi-circle of a beach, and always the
white houses gathered like nests wherever there was the shelter
of a small harbor. Now at last they were approaching the steep-
est, the most dramatic harbor of them all—Santorini. Of course
she had chosen Santorini because it is as inaccessible and remote
as a dream.

This island is guarded by the sinister hump of the barren,
coal-black volcano, which erupted some years ago and, in the en-
suing quake, buried half the village in the sea. The sheer cliff on
which the new village stands is really the lip of a crater, looking
down on the dangerous Cerberus which guards and threatens it.
Already, from her vantage point, Joanna could see the narrow
zig-zagging path, twisting up from the cluster of buildings on the
quay, to the village itself far away on the height. Here within the
deep harbor, the water was magically still, and the whole dramatic scene composed itself in flat planes like a painting. It looked
hardly real. But the roar of the anchor grinding down was real
enough, and Joanna ran back to collect her luggage, to be ready to
disembark into the small boat already close to the ship's ladder.

She was in a sea daze, and the quay seemed to rock slightly as
she stood there, bewildered for a moment among the shouts and
cries of the donkey drivers already competing for the five or six
passengers who had disembarked. She stood there, bewildered,
beside her pile of luggage, smiling at the sight of so many donkeys, donkeys of every size, color, each with a different saddle or
bright blanket thrown over him, attended by their masters who
looked, Joanna thought, like delightful bandits in a child's story.

What made her suddenly notice, far down the quay, another scene, so terrible that at first she turned her eyes away? "I have not come here, all this way, to be wrenched apart again, to be wrenched apart by a donkey," she thought and the thought was a prayer, "Please let me not see what I see." But she did see.

What she saw was an infinitesimal gray donkey, the most miserable animal one could imagine, for his whole belly was an open wound; and on the back of this misery two gypsies were loading an enormous wine cask.

At that second, her daze vanished and she strode past the clamor of reputable donkey-drivers without a glance, her eyes blazing. As she drew closer, she could see the hundreds of flies settling like a black film on the great sores, and, worse, the match-stick legs trembling, trembling, as if they would crack under the preposterous burden just forced upon them.

"Murderers!" The word leapt to her lips but she did not utter it. Instead she looked hard at the two men. One was stooped, a harsh stubble of white beard on his face, an old man breathing heavily from the effort of lifting the cask, for a second leaning against it, so Joanna thought the donkey would crumble there and then. The other man had a hateful look of harsh pleasure in what he was doing. He felt her burning eyes upon him and gave her an uneasy, belligerent glance, then spat.

Joanna forced herself to walk two steps forward, and then said quietly, without taking her eyes from his face, "You are going to kill the donkey."

The old man lifted his head and looked at her with dead eyes.

The young man slouched toward her, and spoke in an angry, whining singsong, "He might last to the top," he said, "We'll work him till he drops, and that's that. Do you think we are rich?" He spat again. "We can't afford to keep a sick animal. If he dies, all right, kaput!"

Joanna flinched before the German word. The memories of cruelty and violence swept over her, cruelty about which one could do nothing; she experienced again the corroding poison of helplessness before violence. She felt suddenly weak, as weak as

the donkey. The donkey had no strength, it seemed, even to wag
its tail at the flies. It waited, just barely able to stand, its head
drooping a little. The patience and suffering of the donkey were
awful.

And Joanna, in her weakness, turned away. What could she
do, after all? What use to stay and witness an agony for which
she could do nothing? It was not her business. Then she heard
the whack of a stick, and rage gave her courage. Before she knew
what she was doing, she had seized the stick by one end and
shouted,

"No! No!"

"Leave me alone. I know what I'm doing!" And Joanna felt
the rough stick torn from her hands. The old man was pushing
the miserable beast from behind, and slowly, slowly, the match
stick legs stumbled a step forward.

"I'll buy it!" Joanna said, beside herself. "I'll give you five hundred drachma!" It was the first sum that came into her head—she
had no idea what a donkey cost—but it seemed a lot. It must be
enough, quickly, quickly, before the donkey crumpled up and
died there before her eyes.

The young man said something in a language that she did not
understand, and the old man stopped pushing, and wiped his face
on a dirty rag.

"Five hundred?" the young man mocked her. "Are you
crazy?"

"Six hundred?" she murmured, not taking her eyes from his.
She was caught now. She was a prisoner of their greed, and her
weakness. And they took eight hundred drachma before they lifted the cask off the poor beast, and set it free.

There she was, on the quay, where she had stepped so light-
heartedly only half an hour ago, as if it were now enemy country.
She stood there, shivering, with a dying donkey at her side, and
nowhere to sleep.

"It will be all right," she said, and saw him wince as she laid a
hand gently on his forehead, as if he expected a blow. How hot
his head was, poor beastie! They stood there a few seconds, lean-

ing together like two orphans, and Joanna looked up at the climb ahead with dismay.

"Come," she said, taking the frayed rope in her hands. The donkey followed at once, before she had given the slightest tug, and this was the first sign between them. He followed her to the pile of luggage. If she strapped the easel and canvases to her back, she could manage to carry the suitcases; hiring a donkey was out of the question now . . . besides they had all left. They were half-way up to the village, laughing and talking. Even the gypsies had disappeared.

"I must be mad," she said to the donkey, who stood there, wrapped in his patience. The immensity of what she had under-taken swept over her in a wave. She sensed that here in this poor village where all lived close to poverty, an act such as hers would seem unpleasant, even indecent. Only the very rich could afford such whims. But the joke was on her, for she was not rich. And the truth was that she felt exhaustion before the effort ahead.

"Well, Ulysses, let's go!" She had found a name for the don-key, without even considering the matter. She grasped the two bags and began slowly to climb the winding path upwards. It was not possible to keep hold of the rope, and she soon let it fall, for Ulysses kept close behind her, his ears pointing forwards, and perhaps it was just as well for him that they moved slowly, with frequent halts, while Joanna struggled to recover from each lap with great heavy breaths. "Oh my dear soul," she uttered once, when it looked as if they would never make it to the top: the higher they climbed, the farther there was to go. "Why did I choose Santorini, of all places? We might at least have met each other on a flat island!"

Near the top, they began to see villagers, widows in black with shawls over their heads, who looked with amazement at the approaching caravan, a shameless woman in gaudy pants leading a donkey whom she had neglected to the point of cruelty. Joanna longed to explain, but by now she had no breath even to speak to Ulysses. She just dropped her eyes, and looked at the stones under her feet, counting steps, and resting after every two hundred, to look down at the serene blue harbor, so far below.

The sunlight reflected sharply off the white houses and Joan-na felt dizzy. "I shall have to have some coffee, Ulysses. And find water for you," she said. The thought of coffee led her on, up the last hairpin curve to the final parapet. There she sat down heavi-ly on a stone step, unable to go further. Ulysses stood two steps below her, so it happened that she could look straight into his face for the first time and saw how beautiful and dark his eyes were, rimmed in long lashes; and again she laid a hand gently on his forehead and caressed his soft nose. When she did this, his drooping ears pricked, and he bent his head a little. But unfortu-nately she could also now see, even better than before, how dreadful the sores on his belly were. She brushed a fly away from his right eye, and watched it go and settle on the oozing blood. And she gave a sigh that came from deep down, a sigh in which fear before what she had undertaken, and pity and loathing of the suffering she had witnessed, all came together and lay around her heart like a heavy weight.

Her arrival at Santorini was very different from what she had imagined when she left Athens that morning, but it was com-pletely in character.

Imprints

MARTHA WATERS

Smokey was the first animal I remember talking to. I'd sit on the top rail of his corral saying "What, Smokey, what?" as he snorted and wiggled his lips with some mysterious message for me. He was a huge black horse and I was too little to ride him by myself but I got as close to him as I could and tried to decipher his language. I'm not sure how accurate my interpretations were but he would nuzzle me with his soft nose and listen to my stories, making his own comments along the way. My mother took movies of me riding on Smokey's back when I was three, clinging to the saddle horn while my father walked him around. I don't remember that at all except from the movies, but I do know that by the time I was old enough to take care of Smokey and ride him every day he had been sold. My big brothers were more interested in cars than horses. If we had lived on a farm with a lot of animals to tend it might have been different, daily chores being something we did out of habit and necessity. But we lived in town and Smokey lived by himself in an open lot across the street, with a little shed he could go inside to keep out of bad weather. My brothers sometimes forgot whose turn it was to feed him and it was finally decided that we should find him another home. The best I could do was to name my bicycle Smokey and pretend I was on horseback when I rode out into the country. The land in western Kansas was flat and uninterrupted, like looking out to sea, and I loved to watch the wind push giant banks of thunderclouds toward me with a fierce speed that thrilled me every time. I talked to Smokey's ghost, leaning into the stiff breeze as I watched him race across the sky in every dark cloud.

◆

Princess was the puppy given to me when I was ten years old, shortly after my father died. Her coat smelled like scrambled eggs when it got wet and Princess was always getting wet. She liked to dive into puddles and bound happily up to me, dripping mud or shaking her whole body from head to tail—an intense tremor that always impressed me even though it got me all wet, too. She followed me everywhere, sat under my chair at the kitchen table and slept with me every night. I told her all my secrets in great detail and was convinced that she used her ears to communicate her responses. Only I could read what they were saying. She would answer my questions by moving her ears in all directions, then freeze them suddenly in some odd position until I spoke again. Sometimes one of them got turned inside out and stayed that way for hours, draped across the back of her head to reveal the pink hole of her inner ear. I imagined this as her way of challenging me with a secret code and sometimes I put both her ears back on purpose so she could speak in a different language entirely. She was a mixture of many breeds with the coloring of a black Lab, the face of a beagle and the small size of a terrier. She adored me and would do anything I asked even if it was danger-ous. I made her sit in my bicycle basket once, instead of trotting along beside me like she usually did, and she obliged for a block or two. Then I went too fast and she got scared, jumped out and hurt her leg in the fall. I was horrified to think that my stupid game had caused pain to my best friend and I winced every time she limped. But she forgave me instantly.

One Christmas my cousin wrapped up a present for Princess and put it under the tree. It was four little red rubber boots and I strapped them to her paws. She was not quite sure what to do with her feet, as though she had forgotten how to walk. I coaxed her across the room and she struggled to come to me, throwing each leg straight out to the side and hesitating before each step. It took her a long time to move a few yards and everyone got a big laugh out of her confusion. I felt so sorry for her that I promised I would never make her wear the boots again.

Chuck was my pet raccoon. He thought I was his mother because I fed him from a doll's baby bottle before his eyes were open and he never had contact with any other raccoons for the first few years of his life. My sister's boyfriend had gone hunting and killed Chuck's mother. When he discovered the baby raccoons he brought them back to town and tried to find homes for them. I begged my mother to let me keep one and she did, even though she had her doubts. She worried that I would become too attached to him and he probably wouldn't live very long. Instead, Chuck quickly grew into a huge, healthy raccoon who loved to climb trees with me and go for long walks. When he got tired he rested by draping himself over my shoulder, gently stroking my cheek with his little black fingers to get me to look at him. He chattered constantly whether I listened or not and seemed to have something to say about everything he saw. He got along just fine with Princess, which really surprised me since I thought dogs and raccoons were natural enemies.

I was an excellent caretaker for about a year but then I became busy with other things and started leaving Chuck alone in his little cabin in the back yard. It was a playhouse my father had built years ago but nobody used it anymore. I kept Chuck locked up inside, bringing him food and water twice a day. He wasn't that interested in eating—what he wanted most was someone to play with and talk to. He grew so lonely that my mother finally decided we should let him go. Our neighbors down the road had offered to take him and they chained him to a tree in their back yard. He lived in a hole about eight feet up the trunk and I went to visit him once but he looked at me like he didn't even know who I was. I was crushed to think he could have forgotten me like that. Then the guilt of what I had done hit me with the force of a tornado and I realized I was responsible for his suffering. People tried to tell me that raccoons just naturally turn mean when they get older and that's the trouble with trying to tame a wild animal. But I think *I* was the one who turned mean, not Chuck, and I'm not at all proud of that fact.

◆

Emma was self-contained from the beginning and refused to respond to me when I was lonely and longed for a lap cat. She was a young stray, totally black in color, and was my first companion when I started living in an apartment of my own. She was beautiful and she knew it better than anyone. I always wanted to find her as soon as I got home from work so I could tell her about my day, but she was never interested and pulled away from me if I tried to pick her up. Emma was insulted that I treated her like a dog sometimes, expecting her to appreciate affection whenever I poured it on her, or wanting her to do tricks to entertain me when I was bored. It took her six months to train me how to love her properly and I could always tell when I had overstepped the species line. She would observe me from a distance with the concentration of an umpire, poised to report any infraction of the rules. I eventually faced the fact that she had no desire to be near me until I was first willing to sit still for a minimum of two hours. Then she would surprise me with a sudden appearance on the arm of my chair as she pretended to be curious about whatever I had in my hands—usually a book. As long as I didn't make a fuss she would stay, hunching down to take a nap. When she was ready, she would either leave abruptly or slip into my lap and position herself carefully between my face and my book. Then she'd look off into the distance behind my head for a while and treat me like a convenient thing to sit on, nothing more. When— and if—she started purring, I came to understand that it was now finally the right time to pet her. She liked to be scratched on the head but she didn't like for her coat to be rubbed the wrong way; she didn't like me to touch her feet but she did like a long, even stroke down the length of her body, letting me tug gently on her tail as I straightened it. I moved slowly and talked quietly while I experimented with new ways to please her, trying to prolong the rare chance to show my intimate respect for such an independent partner.

◆

The doe was only about 30 yards away when I realized that the noise of my moped had confused her. Several other deer were grazing in the opposite field and she had crossed the road ahead of them. Instead of continuing on into the woods, she stood in the ditch and stared at me as I approached. When we were side by side she bolted as though a gun had been fired and we were racing toward a finish line. She could have beaten me easily, her leaps far exceeding my slow pace, but she held herself back and never took her eyes off me. I was not prepared when she hesi- tated for a second and then tried to cross in front of me—it was the last thing I expected her to do. We collided, her shoulders rolling into the front wheel of my moped and knocking it to the ground. She fell and I landed on top of her. For a fraction of a sec- ond I held her body in my arms and I could feel her heart beating through her tight skin like a velvet jackhammer. Her fear brought a musky dampness to the air, both of us gasping in disbelief. In an instant she was out from under me with a great scrambling of legs and feet, darting away to rejoin her kin. I could tell by the way the doe was running that she would be fine once she got over the scare. She disappeared into some trees and I sent a message that no harm was intended and I was sorry for the intrusion. My hands were bleeding but I knew I was not injured. If I could get my moped started again I could get home before dark.

"The Author of the Acacia Seeds" and Other Extracts from the *Journal of the Association of Therolinguistics*

URSULA K. Le GUIN

MS. Found in an Ant-Hill

The messages were found written in touch-gland exudation on degerminated acacia seeds laid in rows at the end of a narrow, erratic tunnel leading off from one of the deeper levels of the colony. It was the orderly arrangement of the seeds that first drew the investigator's attention. The messages are fragmentary, and the translation approximate and highly interpretative; but the text seems worthy of interest if only for its striking lack of resemblance to any other Ant texts known to us.

> SEEDS 1-13
> [I will] not touch feelers. [I will] not stroke. [I will] spend on dry seeds [my] soul's sweetness. It may be found when [I am] dead. Touch this dry wood! [I] call! [I am] here!

Alternatively, this passage may be read:

> [Do] not touch feelers. [Do] not stroke. Spend on dry seeds [your] soul's sweetness. [Others] may

find it when [you are] dead. Touch this dry wood!
Call: [I am] here!

No known dialect of Ant employs any verbal person except the third person singular and plural, and the first person plural. In this text, only the root-forms of the verbs are used; so there is no way to decide whether the passage was intended to be an autobiography or a manifesto.

> SEEDS 14-22
> Long are the tunnels. Longer is the untunneled. No
> tunnel reaches the end of the untunneled. The un-
> tunneled goes on farther than we can go in ten
> days [i.e., forever]. Praise!

The mark translated "Praise!" is half of the customary saluta-tion "Praise the Queen!" or "Long live the Queen!" or "Huzza for the Queen!"—but the word/mark signifying "Queen" has been omitted.

> SEEDS 23-29
> As the ant among foreign-enemy ants is killed, so
> the ant without ants dies, but being without ants
> is as sweet as honeydew.

An ant intruding in a colony not its own is usually killed. Isolated from other ants it invariably dies within a day or so. The difficulty in this passage is the word/mark "without ants," which we take to mean "alone"—a concept for which no word/mark exists in Ant.

> SEEDS 30-31
> Eat the eggs! Up with the Queen!

There has already been considerable dispute over the inter-pretation of the phrase on Seed 31. It is an important question, since all the preceding seeds can be fully understood only in the light cast by this ultimate exhortation. Dr. Rosbone ingeniously argues that the author, a wingless neuter-female worker, yearns hopelessly to be a winged male, and to found a new colony, flying upward in the nuptial flight with a new Queen. Though the text

certainly permits such a reading, our conviction is that nothing in
the text *supports* it – least of all the text of the immediately
preceding seed, No. 30: "Eat the eggs!" This reading, though
shocking, is beyond disputation.

We venture to suggest that the confusion over Seed 31 may
result from an ethnocentric interpretation of the word "up." To
us, "up" is a "good" direction. Not so, or not necessarily so, to an
ant. "Up" is where the food comes from, to be sure; but "down" is
where security, peace, and home are to be found. "Up" is the
scorching sun; the freezing night; no shelter in the beloved tunnels; exile; death. Therefore we suggest that this strange author,
in the solitude of her lonely tunnel, sought with what means she
had to express the ultimate blasphemy conceivable to an ant, and
that the correct reading of Seeds 30-31, in human terms is:

Eat the eggs! Down with the Queen!

The desicated body of a small worker was found beside Seed
31 when the manuscript was discovered. The head had been severed from the thorax, probably by the jaws of a soldier of the colony. The seeds, carefully arranged in a pattern resembling a
musical stave, had not been disturbed. (Ants of the soldier caste
are illiterate; thus the soldier was presumably not interested in
the collection of useless seeds from which the edible germs had
been removed.) No living ants were left in the colony, which was
destroyed in a war with a neighboring ant-hill at some time subse-
quent to the death of the Author of the Acacia Seeds.

–G. D'Arbay, T.R. Bardol

Announcement of an Expedition

The extreme difficulty of reading Penguin has been very
much lessened by the use of the underwater motion picture
camera. On film it is at least possible to repeat, and to slow
down, the fluid sequences of the script, to the point where, by
constant repetition and patient study, many elements of this
most elegant and lively literature may be grasped, though the
nuances, and perhaps the essence, must forever elude us.

It was Professor Duby who, by pointing out the remote affiliation of the script with Low Graylag, made possible the first, tentative glossary of Penguin. The analogies with Dolphin which had been employed up to that time never proved very useful, and were often quite misleading.

Indeed it seemed strange that a script written almost entirely in wings, neck, and air, should prove the key to the poetry of short-necked, flipper-winged water-writers. But we should not have found it so strange if we had kept in mind the fact that penguins are, despite all evidence to the contrary, birds.

Because their script resembles Dolphin in *form*, we should never have assumed that it must resemble Dolphin in *content*. And indeed it does not. There is, of course, the same extraordinary wit and the flashes of crazy humor, the inventiveness, and the inimitable grace. In all the thousands of literatures of the Fish stock, only a few show any humor at all, and that usually of a rather simple, primitive sort; and the superb gracefulness of Shark or Tarpon is utterly different from the joyous vigor of all Cetacean scripts. The joy, the vigor, and the humor are all shared by Penguin authors; and, indeed, by many of the finer Seal *auteurs*. The temperature of the blood is a bond. But the construction of the brain, and of the womb, makes a barrier! Dolphins do not lay eggs. A world of difference lies in that simple fact.

Only when Professor Duby reminded us that penguins are birds, that they do not swim but *fly in water,* only then could the therolinguist begin to approach the sea-literature of the penguin with understanding; only then could the miles of recordings already on film be re-studied and, finally, appreciated.

But the difficulty of translation is still with us.

A satisfying degree of progress has already been made in Adelie. The difficulties of recording a group kinetic performance in a stormy ocean as thick as pea-soup with plankton at a temperature of 31°F are considerable; but the perseverance of the Ross Ice Barrier Literary Circle has been fully rewarded with such passages as "Under the Iceberg," from the *Autumn Song*—a passage now world famous in the rendition of Anna Serebryakova of the Leningrad Ballet. No verbal rendering can approach the felicity of Miss Serebryakova's version. For, quite simply, there is no way to reproduce in writing the all-important *multiplicity* of the original text, so beautifully rendered by the full chorus of the Leningrad Ballet company. Indeed, what we call "translations" from the Adelie—or from any group kinetic text— are, to put it bluntly, mere notes—libretto without the opera. The ballet version is the true translation. Nothing in words can be complete.

I therefore suggest, though the suggestion may well be greeted with frowns of anger or with hoots of laughter, that for the therolinguist—as opposed to the artist and the amateur—the kinetic sea-writings of Penguin are the *least* promising field of study: and, further, that Adelie, for all its charm and relative simplicity, is a less promising field of study than is Emperor.

Emperor!—I anticipate my colleagues' response to this suggestion. Emperor! The most difficult, the most remote, of all the dialects of Penguin! The language of which Professor Duby himself remarked, "The literature of the emperor penguin is as forbidding, as inaccessible, as the frozen heart of Anartica itself. Its beauties may be unearthly, but they are not for us."

Maybe. I do not underestimate the difficulties: not least of which is the Imperial temperament, so much more reserved and aloof than that of any other penguin. But, paradoxically, it is just in this reserve that I place my hope. The emperor is not a solitary, but a social bird, and while on land for the breeding season dwells in colonies, as does the adelie; but these colonies are very much smaller and very much quieter than those of the adelie. The bonds between the members of an emperor colony are rather personal than social. The emperor is an individualist. Therefore I think it almost certain that the literature of the emperor will prove to be composed by single authors, instead of chorally; and therefore it will be translatable into human speech. It will be a kinetic literature, but how different from the spatially extensive, rapid, multiplex choruses of sea-writing! Close analysis, and genuine transcription, will at last be possible.

What! say my critics—Should we pack up and go to Cape Crozier, to the dark, to the blizzards, to the −60° cold, in the mere hope of recording the problematic poetry of a few strange birds who sit there, in the mid-winter dark, in the blizzards, in the −60° cold, on the eternal ice, with an egg on their feet?

And my reply is, Yes. For, like Professor Duby, my instinct tells me that the beauty of that poetry is as unearthly as anything we shall ever find on earth.

To those of my colleagues in whom the spirit of scientific curi-osity and aesthetic risk is strong, I say, imagine it: the ice, the scouring snow, the darkness, the ceaseless whine and scream of wind. In that black desolation a little band of poets crouches. They are starving; they will not eat for weeks. On the feet of each one, under the warm bellyfeathers, rests one large egg, thus preserved from the mortal touch of the ice. The poets cannot hear each other; they cannot see each other. They can only feel the other's *warmth*. That is their poetry, that is their art. Like all kinetic literatures, it is silent; unlike other kinetic literatures, it is all but immobile, ineffably subtle. The ruffling of a feather; the shifting of a wing; the touch, the slight, faint, warm touch of the one beside you. In unutterable, miserable, black solitude, the af-firmation. In absence, presence. In death, life.

I have obtained a sizable grant from UNESCO and have stocked an expedition. There are still four places open. We leave for Antarctica on Thursday. If anyone wants to come along, welcome!

—D. Petri

Editorial by the President of the Therolinguistics Association

What is Language?

This question, central to the science of therolinguists, has been answered—heuristically—by the very existence of the science. Language is communication. That is the axiom on which all our theory and research rest, and from which all our discoveries derive; and the success of the discoveries testifies to the validity of the axiom. But to the related, yet not identical question, What is Art? we have not yet given a satisfactory answer.

Tolstoy, in the book whose title is that very question, answered it firmly and clearly: Art, too, is communication. This answer has, I believe, been accepted without examination or criticism by therolinguistics. For example: Why do therolinguists study only animals?

Why, because plants do not communicate.

Plants do not communicate; that is a fact. Therefore plants have no language; very well; that follows from our basic axiom. Therefore, also, plants have no art. But stay! That does *not* follow from the basic axiom, but only from the unexamined Tolstoyan corollary.

What if art is not communicative?

Or, what if some art is communicative, and some art is not?

Ourselves animals, active, predators, we look (naturally enough) for an active, predatory, communicative art; and when we find it, we recognize it. The development of this power of recognition and the skills of appreciation is a recent and glorious achievement.

But I submit that, for all the tremendous advances made by therolinguistics during the last decades, we are only at the beginning of our age of discovery. We must not become slaves to our own axioms. We have not yet lifted our eyes to the vaster horizons before us. We have not faced the almost terrifying challenge of the Plant.

If a non-communicative, vegetative art exists, we must rethink the very elements of our science, and learn a whole new set of techniques.

For it is simply not possible to bring the critical and technical skills appropriate to the study of Weasel murder-mysteries, or Batrachian erotica, or the tunnel-sagas of the earthworm, to bear on the art of the redwood or the zucchini.

This is proved conclusively by the failure—a noble failure—of the efforts of Dr. Srivas, in Calcutta, using time-lapse photography, to produce a lexicon of Sunflower. His attempt was daring but doomed to failure. For his approach was kinetic—a method appropriate to the *communicative* arts of the tortoise, the oyster, and the sloth. He saw the extreme slowness of the kinesis of plants, and only that, as the problem to be solved.

But the problem was far greater. The art he sought, if it exists, is a non-communicative art: and probably a non-kinetic one. It is possible that Time, the essential element, matrix, and measure of all known animal art, does not enter into vegetable art at all. The plants may use the meter of eternity. We do not know.

We do not know. All we can guess is that the putative Art of the Plant is *entirely different* from the Art of the Animal. What it is, we cannot say; we have not yet discovered it. Yet I predict with some certainty that it exists, and that when it is found it will prove to be, not an action, but a reaction: not a communication, but a reception. It will be exactly the opposite of the art we know and recognize. It will be the first *passive* art known to us. Can we in fact know it? Can we ever understand it?

It will be immensely difficult. That is clear. But we should not despair. Remember that so late as the mid-twentieth century, most scientists, and many artists, did not believe that even Dolphin would ever be comprehensible to the human brain—or worth comprehending! Let another century pass, and we may seem equally laughable. "Do you realize," the phytolinguist will say to the aesthetic critic, "that they couldn't even read Eggplant?" And they will smile at our ignorance, as they pick up their rucksacks and hike on up to read the newly deciphered lyrics of the lichen on the north face of Pike's Peak.

And with them, or after them, may there not come that even bolder adventurer—the first geolinguist, who, ignoring the delicate, transient lyrics of the lichen, will read beneath it the still less communicative, still more passive, wholly atemporal, cold, volcanic poetry of the rocks: each one a word spoken, how long ago, by the earth itself, in the immense solitude, the immenser community, of space.